A VERY
MURDEROUS
CHRISTMAS

Ten Classic Crime Stories for the Festive Season

Margery Allingham · Adrian Conan Doyle
and John Dickson Carr · Anthony Horowitz
G. K. Chesterton · Nicolas Blake
Ruth Rendell · Colin Dexter
Gladys Mitchell · John Mortimer
Edward Hoch

P

PROFILE BOOKS

First published in Great Britain in 2018 by
PROFILE BOOKS LTD
3 Holford Yard
Bevin Way
London WC1X 9HD
www.profilebooks.com

1 3 5 7 9 10 8 6 4 2

Typeset in Fournier by MacGuru Ltd
Printed and bound in Great Britain by
CPI Group (UK) Ltd, Croydon CR0 4YY

A CIP catalogue record for this book is available from the British Library.

ISBN 978 1 78816 101 5
eISBN 978 1 78283 468 7
Book club edition ISBN 978 1 78816 251 7

Mixed Sources
Product group from well-managed
forests and other controlled sources
www.fsc.org Cert no. TT-COC-002227
© 1996 Forest Stewardship Council
FSC

Contents

The Man with the Sack

Margery Allingham

ALBERT DEAR,

We are going to have a quiet family party at home here for the holiday, just ourselves and the dear village. It would be *such fun* to have you with us. There is a train at 10.45 from Liverpool Street which will get you to Chelmsworth in time for us to pick you up for lunch on Christmas Eve. You really must *not* refuse me. Sheila is being rather difficult and I have the Welkins coming. Ada Welkin is a dear woman. Her jewellery is such a responsibility in a house. She *will* bring it. Sheila has invited such an undesirable boy, the son in the Peters crash, absolutely penniless, my dear, and probably quite desperate. As her mother I

1

am naturally anxious. Remember I rely on you.

Affectionately yours,

MAE TURRETT

P.S. Don't bring a car unless you must. The Welkins seem to be bringing two.

Mr Albert Campion, whom most people described as the celebrated amateur criminologist, and who used to refer to himself somewhat sadly as a universal uncle, read the letter a second time before he expressed himself vulgarly but explicitly and pitched it into the waste-paper basket. Then, sitting down at the bureau in the corner of the breakfast-room, he pulled a sheet of notepaper towards him.

'My Dear Mae,' he wrote briefly, 'I can't manage it. You must forgive me. My love to Sheila and George.

Yours ever,

ALBERT.

P.S. My sympathy in your predicament. I think I can put you on to just the man you need: P. Richards, 13 Acacia Border, Chiswick. He is late of the Metropolitan Police and, like myself, is clean, honest and presentable. Your guests' valuables will be perfectly safe while he is in the house and you will find his fee very reasonable.'

He folded the note, sealed it, and addressed it to Lady Turrett, Pharaoh's Court, Pharaoh's Field, Suffolk.

'In other words, my dear Mae,' he said aloud, as he set it on the mantelpiece, 'if you want a private dick in the house, employ one. We are not high-hat, but we have our pride.'

He wandered back to the breakfast-table and the rest of his correspondence. There was another personal letter under the pile of greeting cards sent off a week too soon by earnest citizens who had taken the Postmaster-General's annual warning a shade too seriously, a large blue envelope addressed in a near-printing hand which proclaimed that the writer had gone to her first school in the early nineteen-twenties.

Mr Campion tore it open and a cry from Sheila Turrett's heart fell out.

My Darling Albert,

Please come for Christmas. It's going to be poisonous. Mother has some queer ideas in her head and the Welkins are frightful. Mike is a dear. At least I like him and you will too. He is Mike Peters, the son of the Ripley Peters who had to go to jail when the firm crashed. But it's not Mike's fault, is it? After all, a good many fathers ought to go to jail only they don't get caught. I don't mean George, of course, bless him (you ought to come if only for his sake. He's like a depression leaving the Azores. It's the thought of the Welkins, poor pet). I don't like to ask you to waste your time on our troubles, but Ada Welkin is *lousy* with diamonds and Mother seems to think that Mike might pinch them, his father having been to jail. Darling, if you are faintly decent do come and back us up. After all, it is Christmas.

Yours always (if you come),

Sheila.

P.S. I'm in love with Mike.

For a moment or so Mr Campion sat regarding the letter and its pathetic postscript. Then, rather regretfully, but comforted by a deep sense of virtue, he crossed the room and, tearing up the note he had written to Lady Turrett, settled himself to compose another.

On Christmas Eve the weather decided to be seasonable; a freezing overhead fog turned the city into night and the illuminated shop fronts had the traditional festive appearance even in the morning. It was more than just cold. The damp, soot-laden atmosphere soaked into the bones relentlessly and Mr Campion's recollection of Pharaoh's Court, rising gaunt and bleak amid three hundred acres of ploughed clay and barren salting, all as flat as the estuary beyond, was not enhanced by the chill.

The thought of Sheila and her father cheered him a little, almost but not quite offsetting the prospect of Lady Mae in anxious mood. Buttoning himself into his thickest overcoat, he hoped for the best.

The railway station was a happy pandemonium. Everybody who could not visit the East Coast for the holiday was, it seemed, sending presents there, and Mr Campion, reminded of the custom, glanced anxiously at his suitcase, wondering if the box of cigars for George was too large or the casket of perfume for Mae too modest, if Sheila was still young enough to eat chocolates, and if there would be hordes of unexpected children who would hang round his room wistfully, their mute glances resting upon his barren luggage.

He caught the train with ease, no great feat since it was three-quarters of an hour late, and was sitting in his corner idly watching the excited throng on the platform when he caught sight of Charlie Spring. He recognised the face instantly, but the name came to him slowly from the siftings of his memory.

Jail had done Mr Spring a certain amount of good, Mr Campion reflected as his glance took in the other man's square shoulders and developed chest. He had been a weedy wreck six months ago standing in the big dock at the Old Bailey, the light from the roof shining down upon his small features and his low forehead, beneath which there peered out the stupidest eyes in the world.

At the moment he seemed very pleased with himself, a bad omen for the rest of the community, but Mr Campion was not interested. It was Christmas and he had troubles of his own.

However, from force of habit he made a careful mental note of the man and observed that he had been 'out' for some little time, since he had lost all trace of jail shyness, that temporary fit of nerves which even the most experienced exhibit for a week or so after their release. He saw also that Mr Spring looked about him with the same peculiar brainless cunning which he had exhibited in the dock.

He boarded the train a little lower down and Mr Campion frowned. There was something about Charlie Spring which he had known and which now eluded him. He tried to remember the last and only time he had seen him. He himself had been in court as an expert witness and had heard Mr Spring sentenced for breaking and entering just before his own case had been called. He remembered that it was breaking and entering and he remembered the flat official voice of the police detective who gave evidence.

But there was something else, something definite and personal which kept bobbing about in the back of his mind, escaping him completely whenever he tried to pin it down. It worried him vaguely, as such things do, all the way to Chelmsworth.

Charlie left the train at Ipswich in the company of one hundred and fifty joyous fellow travellers. Mr Campion spotted him as he passed the window, walking swiftly, his head bent and a large new fibre suitcase in his hand.

It occurred to Campion that the man was not dressed in character. He seemed to remember him as a dilapidated but somewhat gaudy figure in a dirty check suit and a pink shirt, whereas at the moment his newish navy greatcoat was a model of sobriety and unobtrusiveness. Still, it was no sartorial peculiarity that haunted his memory. It was something odd about the man, some idiosyncrasy, something slightly funny.

Still faintly irritated, Mr Campion travelled a further ten miles to Chelmsworth. Few country railway stations present a rustic picturesqueness, even in summer, but at any time in the year Chelmsworth was remarkable for its windswept desolation. Mr Campion alighted on to a narrow slab of concrete, artificially raised above the level of the small town in the valley, and drew a draught of heady rain and brine-soaked air into his lungs. He was experiencing the first shock of finding it not unattractive when there was a clatter of brogues on the concrete and a small russet-clad figure appeared before him. He was aware of honey-brown eyes, red cheeks, white teeth, and a stray curl of red hair escaping from a rakish little tweed cap in which a sprig of holly had been pinned.

'Bless you,' said Sheila Turrett fervently. 'Come on. We're hours late for lunch, they'll all be champing like boarding-house pests.'

She linked her arm through his and dragged him along.

'You're more than a hero to come. I am so grateful and so is George. Perhaps it'll start being Christmas now you're here, which it hasn't been so far in spite of the weather. Isn't it glorious?'

Mr Campion was forced to admit that there was a certain exhilaration in the air, a certain indefinable charm in the grey-brown shadows chasing in endless succession over the flat landscape.

'There'll be snow tonight.' The girl glanced up at the featherbed sky. 'Isn't it grand? Christmas always makes me feel so excited. I've got you a present. Remember to bring one for me?'

'I'm your guest,' said Mr Campion with dignity. 'I have a small packet of plain chocolate for you on Christmas morning, but I wished it to be a surprise.'

Sheila climbed into the car. 'Anything will be welcome except diamonds,' she said cheerfully. 'Ada Welkin's getting diamonds, twelve thousand pounds' worth, all to hang round a neck that would disgrace a crocodile. I'm sorry to sound so catty, but we've had these diamonds all through every meal since she came down.'

Mr Campion clambered into the car beside her.

'Dear me,' he said. 'I had hoped for a merry Christmas, peace and goodwill and all that. Village children bursting their little lungs and everybody else's eardrums in their attempts at religious song, while I listened replete with vast quantities of indigestible food.'

Miss Turrett laughed. 'You're going to get your dear little village kids all right,' she said. 'Two hundred and fifty of 'em. Not even Ada Welkin could dissuade Mother from the Pharaoh's Court annual Christmas Eve party. You'll have just time to sleep off your lunch, swallow a cup of tea, and then it's all hands in the music-room. There's the mothers to entertain, too, of course.'

Mr Campion stirred and sighed gently as he adjusted his spectacles.

'I remember now,' he murmured. 'George said something about it once. It's a traditional function, isn't it?'

'More or less.' Sheila spoke absently. 'Mother revived it with modern improvements some years ago. They have a tea and a Christmas tree and a Santa Claus to hand round the presents.'

The prospect seemed to depress her and she relapsed

into gloomy silence as the little car shot over the dry, windswept roads.

Mr Campion regarded her covertly. She had grown into a very pretty girl indeed, he decided, but he hoped the 'son in the Peters crash' was worth the worry he saw in her forehead.

'What about the young gentleman with the erring father?' he ventured diffidently. 'Is he at Pharaoh's Court now?'

'Mike?' She brightened visibly. 'Oh yes, rather. He's been there for the best part of a week. George honestly likes him and I thought for one heavenly moment that he was going to cut the ice with Mother, but that was before the Welkins came. Since then, of course, it hasn't been so easy. They came a day early, too, which is typical of them. They've been here two days already. The son is the nastiest, the old man runs him close and Ada is ghastly.'

'Horrid for them,' said Mr Campion mildly.

Sheila did not smile.

'You'll spot it at once when you see Ada,' she said, 'so I may as well tell you. They're fantastically rich and Mother has been goat-touting. It's got to be faced.'

'Goat-touting?'

Sheila nodded earnestly.

'Yes. Lots of society women do it. You must have seen the little ads in the personal columns: "Lady of title will chaperone young girl or arrange parties for an older woman."

Or "Lady X. would entertain suitable guest for the London season." In other words, Lady X. will tout around any socially ambitious goat in exchange for a nice large, ladylike fee. It's horrid, but I'm afraid that is how Mother got hold of Ada in the first place. She had some pretty heavy bridge losses at one time. George doesn't know a thing about it, of course, poor darling – and mustn't. He'd be so shocked. I don't know how he accounts for the Welkins.'

Mr Campion said nothing. It was like Mae Turrett, he reflected, to visit her sins upon her family. Sheila was hurrying on.

'We've never seen the others before,' she said breathlessly. 'Mother gave two parties for Ada in the season and they had a box at the Opera to show some of the diamonds. I couldn't understand why they wanted to drag the menfolk into it until they got here. Then it was rather disgustingly plain.'

Mr Campion pricked up his ears.

'So nice for the dear children to get to know each other?' he suggested.

Miss Turrett blushed fiercely. 'Something like that,' she said briefly and added after a pause, 'Have you ever met the sort of young man who's been thrust into a responsible position in a business because, and only because, he's Poppa's son? A lordly, blasé sulky young man who's been kow-towed to by subordinates who are fifty times as intelligent as he is himself? The sort of young man you want to kick on sight?'

Mr Campion sighed deeply. 'I have.'

Sheila negotiated a right-angle turn. Her forehead was wrinkled and her eyes thoughtful.

'This'll show you the sort of man Kenneth Welkin is,' she said. 'It's so petty and stupid that I'm almost ashamed to mention it, but it does show you. We've had a rather difficult time amusing the Welkins. They don't ride or shoot or read, so this morning, when Mike and I were putting the final touches to the decorations, we asked Kenneth to help us. There was a stupid business over some mistletoe. Kenneth had been laying down the law about where it was to hang and we were a bit tired of him already when he started a lot of silly horseplay. I don't mind being kissed under the mistletoe, of course, bu – well, it's the way you do these things, isn't it?'

She stamped on the accelerator to emphasise her point, and Mr Campion, not a nervous man, clutched the side of the car.

'Sorry,' said Sheila and went on with her story. 'I tried to wriggle away after a bit, and when he wouldn't let me go Mike suddenly lost his temper and told him to behave himself or he'd damned well knock his head off. It was awfully melodramatic and stupid, but it might have passed off and been forgotten if Kenneth hadn't made a scene.

First he said he wouldn't be talked to like that, and then he made a reference to Mike's father, which was unforgivable. I thought they were going to have a fight. Then, right in the middle of it, Mother fluttered in with a Santa Claus costume. She looked at Mike and said, "You'd better try it on, dear. I want you to be most realistic this afternoon." Before he could reply, Kenneth butted in. He looked like a spoilt kid, all pink and furious. "I didn't know you were going to be Father Christmas," he said.'

Miss Turrett paused for breath, her eyes wide.

'Well, can you imagine anything so idiotic?' she said. 'Mike had offered to do the job when he first came down because he wanted to make himself useful. Like everyone else, he regarded it as a fatigue. It never dawned on him that anyone would *want* to do it. Mother was surprised, too, I think. However, she just laughed and said, "You must fight it out between you" and fluttered away again, leaving us all three standing there. Kenneth picked up the costume. "It's from Harridge's," he said. "My mother was with Lady Mae when she ordered it. I thought it was fixed up then that I was to wear it."'

Mr Campion laughed. He felt very old.

'I suppose Master Michael stepped aside like a little gent and Master Kenneth appears as St Nicholas?' he murmured.

'Well no, not exactly' Sheila sounded a little embarrassed. 'Mike was still angry, you see, because Kenneth really had been infernally casual. He suddenly decided to be obstinate. Mother had asked him to do the job, he said, and he was going to do it. I thought they were going to have an open row about it, which would have been quite too absurd, but at that moment the most idiotic thing of all happened. Old Mr Welkin, who had been prowling about listening as usual, came in and told Kenneth he was to 'give way' to Mike – literally, in so many words! It all sounds perfectly mad now I've told it to you, yet Mike is really rather a darling.'

Mr Campion detected a certain wistfulness in her final phrase and frowned.

Pharaoh's Court looked unexpectedly mellow and inviting as they came up the drive some minutes later. The old house had captured the spirit of the season and Mr Campion stepped out of a cold grey world into an enormous entrance hall where the blaze from the nine-foot hearth flickered on the glossy leaves of the ivy and holly festooned along the carved beams of the ceiling.

George Turrett, grey-haired and cherubic, was waiting for them. He grasped the visitor's hand with fervour. 'So glad you've come,' he murmured. 'Devilish glad to see you, Campion.'

His extreme earnestness was apparent and Sheila put an arm round his neck.

'It's a human face in the wilderness, isn't it, darling?' she murmured.

Sir George's guilty protest was cut short by the first luncheon bell, a reminder that the train had arrived late, and Mr Campion was rushed upstairs to his room by a harassed manservant.

He saw the clock as he came down again a moment or so later. It burst upon him as he turned a corner in the corridor and came upon it standing on a console table. Even in his haste it arrested him. Mae Turrett had something of a reputation for interior decoration, but large country houses have a way of collecting furnishing oddities, however rigorous their owner's taste may be.

Although he was not as a rule over-sensitive to artistic monstrosities, Mr Campion paused in respectful astonishment before this example of the mid-Victorian baroque. A bewildered-looking bronze lady, clad in a pink marble nightgown, was seated upon a gilt ormolu log, one end of which had been replaced by a blue and white enamel clock face. Even as he stared the contraption chimed loudly and aggressively, while downstairs a second luncheon bell rang.

He passed on and forgot all about the clock as soon as he entered the dining-room. Mae Turrett sprang at him with little affected cries which he took to indicate a hostess's delight.

'Albert *dear!*' she said breathlessly. 'How marvellous to see you! Aren't we wonderfully festive? The gardener assures me it's going to snow tonight, in fact he's virtually promised it. I do love a real old family party at Christmas, don't you? Just our very own selves ... too lovely! Let me introduce you to a very dear friend of mine: Mrs Welkin – Mr Campion ...'

Campion was aware of a large middle-aged woman with drooping cheeks and stupid eyes who sniggered at him and looked away again.

Lunch was not a jolly meal by any means. Even Lady Turrett's cultivated chatter died down every now and again. However, Mr Campion had ample opportunity to observe the strangers of whom he had heard so much.

Mike Peters was a surprise to him. He had expected a nervy, highly-strung young man, afflicted, probably, with a generous dose of self-pity, as the innocent victim of his father's misdeeds or misfortunes, but found instead a sturdy silent youngster with a brief smile and a determined chin. It was obvious that he knew what he wanted and was going for it steadily. Mr Campion found himself wishing him luck.

Since much criticism before a meeting may easily defeat its own ends, Mr Campion had been prepared to find the Welkin family pleasant but misunderstood people, round pegs in a very square hole. But here again he was mistaken.

Kenneth Welkin, a fresh-faced, angry-eyed young man in clothes which managed to look expensive while intending to appear nonchalant, sat next to Sheila and sulked throughout the meal. The only remark he addressed to Mr Campion was to ask him what make of car he drove and to disapprove loudly of the answer to his question.

A closer inspection of Mrs Welkin did not dispel Mr Campion's first impression, but her husband interested him. Edward Welkin was a large man with a face that would have been distinguished had it not been for the eyes, which were too shrewd, and the mouth, which was too coarse. His attitude towards his hostess was conspicuously different from his wife's, which was ingratiating, and his son's, which was uneasy and unnecessarily defensive. The most obvious thing about him was that he was complacently alien. George he regarded quite clearly as a nincompoop and Lady Turrett as a woman who so far had given his wife value for money. Of everyone else he was sublimely unconscious.

His plus-fours, of the best Savile Row old-gentleman variety, had their effect ruined by the astonishing quantity of jewellery he chose to display at the same time. He wore two signet rings, one with an agate and one with a sapphire, and an immense jewelled tiepin, while out of his waistcoat pocket peeped a gold and onyx pen with a pencil to match, strapped together in a bright green leather case. They were both of them as thick round as his forefinger and looked at first glance like the insignia of some obscure order.

Just before they rose from the table Mrs Welkin cleared her throat.

'As you're going to have a crowd of *tenants* this evening, Mae, dear, I don't think I'll wear it, do you?' she said with a giggle and a glance at Mr Campion.

'Wear what, dear?' Lady Turrett spoke absently and Mrs Welkin looked hurt.

'The necklace,' she said reverently.

'Your diamonds? Good heavens, no! Most unsuitable.' The words escaped her ladyship involuntarily, but in a moment she was mistress of herself and the situation. 'Wear something very simple,' she said with a mechanical smile. 'I'm afraid it's going to be very hard work for us all. Mike, you do know exactly what to do, don't you? At the end of the evening, just before they go home, you put on the costume and come into the little anteroom which leads off the platform. You go straight up to the tree and cut the presents off, while all the rest of us stand round to receive them and pass them on to the children.'

Mrs Welkin bridled. 'I should have liked to have worn them,' she said irritatingly. 'Still, if you say it's not safe ...'

'Mother didn't say it wasn't safe, Mrs Welkin,' said Sheila, who was fond of the village and resented bitterly any aspersions on its honesty. 'She said it wasn't suitable.'

Mrs Welkin blushed angrily and forgot herself.

'You're not very polite, young lady,' she said, 'and if it's a question of suitability, where's the suitability in Mr Peters playing Santa Claus when it was promised to Kenny?'

The mixture of muddled logic and resentment startled everyone. Mike and Sheila grew scarlet, Sir George looked helplessly at his wife, Kenneth Welkin turned savagely on his mother, and Edward Welkin settled rather than saved the situation.

'That'll do,' he said in a voice of thunder. 'That's all been fixed, Ada. I don't want to hear any more from either of you on the subject.'

It was altogether a very awkward moment and the table broke up with relief. Sir George tugged Campion's arm.

'Cigar – library' he murmured, and faded quietly away. Campion followed him.

There were Christmas decorations in the big book-filled study and, as he settled himself in a wing chair before a fire of logs and attended to the tip of a Romeo y Julieta, Mr Campion felt once more the return of the Christmas spirit.

Sir George was anxious about his daughter's happiness.

'I like young Peters,' he said earnestly. 'Fellow can't help his father's troubles. Mae objects he hasn't any money, but, between you and me, Campion, I'd rather see her in rags tied to a decent fellow than sittin' up in a Rolls-Royce beside that little Welkin bounder in the next room.'

Mr Campion agreed with him and he went on.

'The boy Mike's an engineer,' he said, 'and makin' good at his job slowly, and Sheila seems fond of him, but Mae talks about hereditary dishonesty. Taint may be there. What do you think?'

Mr Campion had no time to reply to this somewhat unlikely theory. There was a flutter and a rustle outside the door and a moment later Mr Welkin senior came in with a flustered lady. George got up and held out his hand.

'Ah, Miss Hare,' he said. 'Glad to see you. Come on your annual visit of mercy?'

Miss Hare, who was large and inclined to be hearty, laughed.

'I've come cadging again, if that's what you mean, Sir George,' she said cheerfully, and went on, nodding to Mr Campion as if they had just been introduced. 'Every Christmas Eve I come round collecting for my old women. There are four of 'em in the almshouse by the church. I only ask for a shilling or two to buy them some little extra for the Christmas dinner. I don't want much. Just a shilling or two.'

She glanced at a little notebook in her hand.

'You gave me ten shillings last year, Sir George.'

The Squire produced the required sum and Mr Campion felt in his pocket.

'Half a crown would be ample,' said Miss Hare encouragingly. 'Oh, that's very nice of you. I assure you it won't be wasted.'

She took the coin and was turning to Welkin when he stepped forward.

'I'd like to do the thing properly,' he said. Anybody got a pen?'

He took out a chequebook and sat down at George's desk uninvited.

Miss Hare protested. 'Oh no, really,' she said, 'you don't understand. This is just for an extra treat. I collect it nearly all in sixpences.'

'Anybody got a pen?' repeated Mr Welkin.

Campion glanced at the elaborate display in the man's own waistcoat pocket, but before he could mention it George had meekly handed over his own fountain pen.

Mr Welkin wrote a cheque and handed it to Miss Hare without troubling to blot it.

'Ten pounds?' said the startled lady. 'Oh, but really …!'

'Nonsense. Run along.' Mr Welkin clapped her familiarly on the shoulder. 'It's Christmas time,' he said, glancing at George and Campion. 'I believe in doing a bit of good at Christmas time – if you can afford it.'

Miss Hare glanced round her helplessly.

'It's very – very kind of you,' she murmured, 'but half a crown would have been ample.'

She fled. Welkin threw George's pen on the desk.

'That's the way I like to do it,' he said.

George coughed and there was a faraway expression in his eyes.

'Yes, I – er – I see you do,' he said and sat down. Welkin went out.

Neither Mr Campion nor his host mentioned the incident. Campion frowned. Now he had two minor problems on his conscience. One was the old matter of the little piece of information concerning Charlie Spring which he had forgotten, the other was a peculiarity of Mr Welkin's which puzzled him mightily.

The Pharaoh's Court children's party had been in full swing for what seemed to Mr Campion at least to be the best part of a fortnight. It was half-past seven in the evening and the relics of an enormous tea had been cleared away, leaving the music-room full of replete but still energetic children and their mothers, dancing and playing games with enthusiasm, but their eyes never straying for long from the next sensation of the evening, the fourteen-foot tree ablaze with coloured lights and tinsel.

Mr Campion, who had danced, buttled, and even performed a few conjuring tricks, bethought him of a box of his favourite cigarettes in his suitcase upstairs and, feeling only a little guilty at leaving George still working like a hero, he stole away and hurried up the deserted staircase to his room.

The main body of the house was deserted. Even the Welkins were at work in the music-room, while the entire staff were concentrated in the kitchen washing up.

Mr Campion found his cigarettes, lit one, and pottered for a moment or two, reflecting that the Christmases of his youth were much the same as those of today, but not so long from hour to hour. He felt virtuous and happy and positively oozing with goodwill. The promised snow was falling, great soft flakes plopping softly against his window.

At last, when his conscience decreed that he could absent himself no longer, he switched off the light and stepped into the corridor, to come unexpectedly face to face with Father Christmas. The saint looked as weary as he himself had been and was stooping under the great sack on his shoulders. Mr Campion admired Harridge's costume. The boots were glossy, the tunic with its wool border satisfyingly red, while the benevolent mask with its cotton-wool beard was almost lifelike.

He stepped aside to let the venerable figure pass and, because it seemed the moment for jocularity, said lightly:

'What have you got in the bag, Guv'nor?'

Had he uttered a spell of high enchantment, the simple words could not have had a more astonishing effect. The figure uttered an inarticulate cry, dropped the sack, which fell with a crash at Mr Campion's feet, and fled like a shadow.

For a moment Mr Campion stood paralysed with astonishment. By the time he had pulled himself together the crimson figure had disappeared down the staircase. He bent over the sack and thrust in his hand. Something hard and heavy met his fingers and he brought it out. It was the pink marble, bronze and ormolu clock.

He stood looking at his find and a sigh of satisfaction escaped him. One of the problems that had been worrying him all day had been solved at last.

It was twenty minutes later before he reappeared in the music-room.

No one saw him come in, for the attention of the entire room was focused upon the platform. There, surrounded by enthusiastic assistants, was Father Christmas again, peacefully snipping presents off the tree.

Campion took careful stock of him. The costume, he decided, was identical, the same high boots, the same tunic, the same mask. He tried to remember the fleeting figure in the corridor upstairs, but the costume was a deceptive one and he found it difficult.

After a time he found a secluded chair and sat down to await developments. They came.

As the last of the visitors departed, tired and smiling, their coats buttoned against the snow, and Lady Turrett threw herself into an armchair with a sigh of happy exhaustion, Pouter, the Pharaoh's Court butler, came quietly into the room and murmured a few words in his master's ear. From where he sat Mr Campion heard George's astonished 'God bless my soul!' and rose immediately to join him. But although he moved swiftly Mr Welkin was before him and, as Campion reached the group, his voice resounded round the room.

'A burglary? While we've been playing the fool in here? What's gone, man? What's gone?'

Pouter, who for some obscure reason of his own objected to the form of address, regarded his master's guest coldly.

'A clock from the first floor west corridor, a silver-plated salver, a copper loving-cup from the hall, and a brass Buddha and a gilt pomander box from the first-floor landing, as far as we can ascertain, sir,' he said.

'Bless my soul!' said George again. 'How extraordinary!'

'Extraordinary be damned!' ejaculated Welkin. 'We've got *valuables* here. Ada!'

'The necklace!' shrieked Mrs Welkin, consternation suddenly welling up in her stupid eyes. 'My necklace!'

She scuttled out of the room and Sheila came forward

with Santa Claus, who had taken off his mask and pushed back his hood to reveal the stolid but not unhandsome features of Mike Peters.

Lady Turrett did not stir from her chair, and Kenneth Welkin, white-faced and bewildered, stared down at her.

'There's been a burglary,' he said. 'Here, in this house.'

Mae Turrett smiled at him vaguely. 'George and Pouter will see to it,' she said. 'I'm so tired.'

'Tired!' shouted Edward Welkin. 'If my wife's diamonds—'

He got no further. Ada Welkin tottered into the room, an empty steel dispatch case in her trembling hands.

'They've gone,' she said, her voice rising in hysteria. 'They've gone. My diamonds … My room's been turned upside down. They've been taken. The necklace has gone.'

It was Mike who had sufficient presence of mind to support her to a chair before she collapsed. Her husband shot a shrewd, preoccupied glance at her, shouted to his son to 'Look after your mother, boy!' and took command of the situation.

'Now this is serious. You, Pigeon, whatever your name is, get all the servants, everyone who's in this house, to come here in double-quick time, see? I've been robbed.'

Pouter looked at his master in mute appeal and George coughed.

'In a moment, Mr Welkin,' he said. 'In a moment. Let us find out what we can first. Pouter, go and find out if any stranger has been seen about the house or grounds this evening, will you, please?'

The manservant went out instantly and Welkin raged.

'You may think you know what you're doing,' he said, but my way was the best. You're giving the thief time to get away, and time's precious, let me tell you. I've got to get the police up here.'

'The police?' Sheila was aghast.

He gaped at her. 'Of course, young woman. Do you think I'm going to lose twelve thousand pounds? The stones were insured, of course, but what company would pay up if I hadn't called in the police? I'll go and 'phone up now.'

'Wait a moment, please,' said George, his quiet voice only a little ruffled. 'Here's Pouter again. Well?'

The butler looked profoundly uncomfortable.

'Two maids, sir,' he said, 'the under housemaid and Miss Sheila's maid, Lucy, were waiting in the hall to tell me that they saw a man running down the drive just before the Christmas tree was begun.' He hesitated. 'They— they say, sir, he was dressed as Father Christmas. They both say it, sir.' Everyone looked at Mike and Sheila's cheeks flamed. 'Well?' she demanded.

Mr Welkin suddenly laughed. 'So that's how it was done,' he said. 'The young blackguard was clever, but he was seen. You weren't so bright as you thought you were, my lad.'

Mike moved forward. His face was pale and his eyes were dangerous. George laid a hand upon his arm.

'Wait,' he commanded. 'Pouter, you may go. Now,' he continued as the door closed behind the man, 'you, Mr Welkin, you'll have to explain, you know.'

Mr Welkin kept his temper. He seemed almost amused. 'Well, it's perfectly simple, isn't it?' he said. 'This fellow has been wandering about in this disguise all the evening. He couldn't come in here because her ladyship wanted him to be a surprise to the children, but he had the rest of the house to himself. He went round lifting anything he fancied, including my diamonds. Suppose he had been met? No one would think anything of it. Father Christmas always carries a sack. Then he went off down the drive, where he met a confederate in a car, handed over the stuff and came back to the party'

Mike began to speak, but Sheila interrupted him. 'What makes you think Mike would do such a thing, Mr Welkin?' she demanded, her voice shaking with fury.

Edward Welkin's heavy mouth widened in a grin. 'Dishonesty's in the family, isn't it?' he said.

Mike sprang, but George clung to him. 'Hold on, my boy, hold on,' he said breathlessly. 'Don't strike a man old enough to be your—'

He boggled at the unfortunate simile and substituted the word 'mother' with ludicrous effect.

Mr Campion decided it was time to interfere.

'I say, George,' he said, 'if you and Mr Welkin would come along to the library I've got a suggestion I'd like to make.'

Welkin wavered. 'Keep an eye on him then, Ken,' he said over his shoulder to his son. I'll listen to you, Campion, but I want my diamonds back and I want the police. I'll give you five minutes, no longer.'

The library was in darkness when the three men entered, and Campion waited until they were well in the room before he switched on the main light. There was a moment of bewildered silence. One corner of the room looked like a stall in the Caledonian Market. There the entire contents of the sack, which had come so unexpectedly into Mr Campion's possession, was neatly spread out. George's cherubic face darkened.

'What's this?' he demanded. 'A damned silly joke?'

Mr Campion shook his head. 'I'm afraid not. I've just collected this from a gentleman in fancy dress whom I met in the corridor upstairs,' he said. 'What would you say, Mr Welkin?'

The man stared at him doggedly. 'Where are my diamonds? That's my only interest. I don't care about this junk.'

Campion smiled faintly. 'He's right, you know, George,' he said. 'Junk's the word. It came back to me as soon as I saw it. Poor Charlie Spring – I recognised him, Mr Welkin – never had a successful coup in his life because he can't help stealing gaudy junk.'

Edward Welkin stood stiffly by the desk.

'I don't understand you,' he said. 'My diamonds have been stolen and I want to call the police.'

Mr Campion took off his spectacles. 'I shouldn't if I were you,' he said. 'No you don't—!'

On the last words Mr Campion leapt forward and there was a brief struggle. When it was over Mr Welkin was lying on the floor beside the marble and ormolu clock and Mr Campion was grasping the gold pen and pencil in the leather holder which until a moment before had rested in the man's waistcoat pocket.

Welkin scrambled to his feet. His face was purple and his eyes a little frightened. He attempted to bluster.

'You'll find yourself in court for assault,' he said. 'Give me my property.'

'Certainly. All of it,' agreed Mr Campion obligingly. 'Your dummy pen, your dummy pencil, and in the little receptacle which they conceal, your wife's diamonds.'

On the last word he drew the case apart and a glittering string fell out in his hand.

There was a long, long pause.

Welkin stood sullenly in the middle of the room.

'Well?' he said at last. 'What are you two going to do about it?'

Mr Campion glanced at George, who was sitting by the desk, an expression of incredulity amounting almost to stupefaction upon his mild face.

'If I might suggest,' he murmured, 'I think he might take his family and spend a jolly Christmas somewhere else, don't you? It would save a lot of trouble.'

Welkin held out his hand.

'Very well. I'll take my diamonds.'

Mr Campion shook his head. 'As you go out of the house,' he said with a faint smile. 'I shouldn't like them to be – lost again.'

Welkin shrugged his shoulders. 'You win,' he said briefly. I'll go and tell Ada to pack.'

He went out of the room, and as the door closed behind him George bounced to his feet.

'Hanged if I understand it …' he began. 'D'you mean to say the feller put up this amazing cock-and-bull story simply so that he could get Mike accused of theft?'

Mr Campion remained serious. 'Oh no,' he said. 'That was an artistic afterthought, I imagine. The cock-and-bull story, as you call it, was a very neat little swindle devised by our unpleasant friend before he came down here at all. It was very simple to stage a burglary here on Christmas

Eve, especially when he had heard from his wife that Mae had ordered a Santa Claus costume from Harridge's. All he had to do was to go and get one there too. Then, armed with the perfect disguise, he enlisted the services of a genuine burglar, to whom he gave the costume. The man simply had to walk into the house, pick up a few things at random, and go off with them. I think you'll find if you go into it that he hired a car at Ipswich and drove out here, changing somewhere along the road.'

George was still puzzled. 'But his own son Kenneth was going to play Santa Claus,' he said. 'Or at least he seemed to expect to.'

Campion nodded. 'I know,' he said. 'Welkin had foreseen that difficulty and prepared for it. If Kenneth had been playing Father Christmas and the same thing had happened I think you would have found that the young man had a pretty convincing alibi established for him. You must remember the burglar was not meant to be seen. He was only furnished with the costume in case he was. As it happened, of course, when Welkin *père* saw that Mike was not too unlike his burglar friend in build, he encouraged the change-over and killed two birds with one stone – or tried to.'

His host took the diamonds and turned them over. He was slow of comprehension.

'Why steal his own property?' he demanded.

Mr Campion sighed. 'You have such a blameless mind,

George, that the wickedness of some of your fellow men must be a constant source of astonishment to you,' he murmured. 'Did you hear our friend Welkin say that he had insured this necklace?'

George's eyebrows rose.

'God bless my soul!' he said. 'The bounder! In our house too,' he added as an afterthought. 'Miracle you spotted it, Campion. God bless my soul! Draw the insurance and keep the diamonds … Damnable trick.'

He was still wrathful when the door burst open and Mae Turrett came in, followed by Mike and Sheila.

'The Welkins are going. They've ordered their cars. What on earth's happened, George?'

Her ladyship was startled but obviously relieved.

Mr Campion explained. 'It had been worrying me all day' he said after the main part of the story had been told. 'I knew Charlie Spring had a peculiarity, but I couldn't think what it was until I pulled that clock out of the bag. Then I remembered his penchant for the baroque and his sad habit of mistaking it for the valuable. That ruled out the diamonds instantly. They wouldn't be big enough for Charlie. When that came back to me I recollected his other failing. He never works alone. When Mr Spring appears on a job it always means he has a confederate in the house, usually an employee, and with these facts in my hand the rest was fairly obvious.'

Mike moved forward. 'You've done me a pretty good turn, anyway' he said.

George looked up. 'Not really, my boy' he said. 'We're not utter fools, you know, are we Mae?'

Lady Turrett blushed. 'Of course not, Mike my dear,' she said, and her smile could be very charming. 'Take Sheila away and cheer her up. I really don't think you need wait about to say goodbye to the Welkins. Dear me, I seem to have been very silly!'

Before she went out Sheila put her hand into Mr Campion's.

'I told you I was glad to see you,' she said.

As the two cars containing the Welkins, their diamonds and all that was theirs disappeared down the white drive, George linked his arm through Mr Campion's and led him back to the library.

'I've been thinking,' he said. 'You spotted that pen was a dummy when Miss Hare came in this afternoon.'

Mr Campion grinned. 'Well, it was odd the man didn't use his own pen, wasn't it?' he said, settling himself before the fire. 'When he ignored it I guessed. That kind of cache is fairly common, especially in the States. They're made for carrying valuables and are usually shabby Bakelite things which no one would steal in the ordinary way. However, there was nothing shabby about Mr Welkin – except his behaviour.'

George leant back in his chair and puffed contentedly.

'Difficult feller,' he observed. 'Didn't like him from the first. No conversation. I started him on shootin', but he wasn't interested, mentioned huntin' and he gaped at me, went on to fishin' and he yawned. Couldn't think of anything to talk to him about. Feller hadn't any conversation at all.'

He smiled and there was a faintly shamefaced expression in his eyes.

'Campion,' he said softly.

'Yes?'

'Made a wonderful discovery last week.' George had lowered his voice to a conspiratorial rumble. 'Went down to the cellar and found a single bottle of Cockburn's 'sixty-eight. 'Sixty-eight, my boy! My father must have missed it. I was saving it for tomorrow, don't you know, but whenever I looked at that feller Welkin, I couldn't feel hospitable. Such a devilish waste. However, now he's gone—' His voice trailed away.

'A very merry Christmas indeed,' supplemented Mr Campion.

The Adventure of the Red Widow

Adrian Conan Doyle & John Dickson Carr

'Your conclusions are perfectly correct, my dear Watson,' remarked my friend Sherlock Holmes. 'Squalor and poverty are the natural matrix to crimes of violence.'

'Precisely so,' I agreed. 'Indeed, I was just thinking—' I broke off to stare at him in amazement. 'Good heavens, Holmes,' I cried, 'this is too much. How could you possibly know my innermost thoughts!'

My friend leaned back in his chair and, placing his finger-tips together, surveyed me from under his heavy, drooping eyelids.

'I would do better justice, perhaps, to my limited powers by refusing to answer your question,' he said, with a dry

chuckle. 'You have a certain flair, Watson, for concealing your failure to perceive the obvious by the cavalier
manner in which you invariably accept the explanation of
a sequence of simple but logical reasoning.'

'I do not see how logical reasoning can enable you to
follow the course of my mental processes,' I retorted, a
trifle nettled by his superior manner.

'There was no great difficulty. I have been watching
you for the last few minutes. The expression on your face
was quite vacant until, as your eyes roved about the room,
they fell on the bookcase and came to rest on Hugo's *Les
Miserables* which made so deep an impression upon you
when you read it last year. You became thoughtful, your
eyes narrowed, it was obvious that your mind was drift-
ing again into that tremendous dreadful saga of human
suffering; at length your gaze lifted to the window with its
aspect of snowflakes and grey sky and bleak, frozen roofs,
and then, moving slowly on to the mantelpiece, settled on
the jack-knife with which I skewer my unanswered correspondence. The frown darkened on your face and unconsciously you shook your head despondently. It was an
association of ideas. Hugo's terrible sub-third stage, the
winter cold of poverty in the slums and, above the warm
glow of our own modest fire, the bare knife-blade. Your
expression deepened into one of sadness, the melancholy
that comes with an understanding of cause and effect in

the unchanging human tragedy. It was then that I ventured to agree with you.'

'Well, I must confess that you followed my thoughts with extraordinary accuracy,' I admitted. 'A remarkable piece of reasoning, Holmes.'

'Elementary, my dear Watson.'

The year of 1887 was moving to its end. The iron grip of the great blizzards that commenced in the last week of December had closed on the land and beyond the windows of Holmes's lodgings in Baker Street lay a gloomy vista of grey, lowering sky and white-capped tiles dimly discernible through a curtain of snowflakes.

Though it had been a memorable year for my friend, it had been of yet greater importance to me, for it was but two months since that Miss Mary Morston had paid me the signal honour of joining her destiny to mine. The change from my bachelor existence as a half-pay, ex-Army surgeon into the state of wedded bliss had not been accomplished without some uncalled-for and ironic comments from Sherlock Holmes but, as my wife and I could thank him for the fact that we had found each other, we could afford to accept his cynical attitude with tolerance and even understanding.

I had dropped in to our old lodgings on this afternoon, to be precise December 30th, to pass a few hours with my friend and enquire whether any new case of interest had come his way since my previous visit. I had found him pale and listless, his dressing-gown drawn round his shoulders and the room reeking with the smoke of his favourite black shag, through which the fire in the grate gleamed like a brazier in a fog.

'Nothing, save a few routine enquiries, Watson,' he had replied in a voice shrill with complaint. 'Creative art in crime seems to have become atrophied since I disposed of the late-lamented Bert Stevens.' Then, lapsing into silence, he curled himself up morosely in his armchair, and not another word passed between us until my thoughts were suddenly interrupted by the observation that commenced this narrative.

As I rose to go, he looked at me critically.

'I perceive, Watson,' said he, 'that you are already paying the price. The slovenly state of your left jaw-bone bears regrettable testimony that somebody has changed the position of your shaving-mirror. Furthermore, you are indulging in extravagances.'

'You do me a gross injustice.'

'What, at the winter price of fivepence a blossom! Your buttonhole tells me that you were sporting a flower not later than yesterday.'

'This is the first time I have known you penurious, Holmes,' I retorted with some bitterness.

He broke into a hearty laugh. 'My dear fellow, you must

forgive me!' he cried. 'It is most unfair that I should pen-alise you because a surfeit of unexpended mental energy tends to play upon my nerves. But hullo, what's this!'

A heavy step was mounting the stairs. My friend waved me back into my chair.

'Stay a moment, Watson,' said he. 'It is Gregson, and the old game may be afoot once more.'

'Gregson?'

'There is no mistaking that regulation tread. Too heavy for Lestrade's and yet known to Mrs Hudson or she would accompany him. It is Gregson.'

As he finished speaking, there came a knock on the door and a figure muffled to the ears in a heavy cape entered the room. Our visitor tossed his bowler on the nearest chair and unwinding the scarf wrapped around the lower part of his face, disclosed the flaxen hair and long, pale fea-tures of the Scotland Yard detective.

'Ah, Gregson,' greeted Holmes, with a sly glance in my direction. 'It must be urgent business that brings you out in this inclement weather. But throw off your cape, man, and come over to the fire.'

The police-agent shook his head. 'There is not a moment to lose,' he replied, consulting a large silver turnip watch. 'The train to Derbyshire leaves in half an hour and I have a hansom waiting below. Though the case should present no difficulties for an officer of my experi-ence, nevertheless I shall be glad of your company.'

'Something of interest?'

'Murder, Mr Holmes,' snapped Gregson curtly, 'and a singular one at that, to judge from the telegram from the local police. It appears that Lord Jocelyn Cope, the Deputy-Lieutenant of the County, has been found butchered at Arnsworth Castle. The Yard is quite capable of solving crimes of this nature, but in view of the curious terms contained in the police telegram, it occurred to me that you might wish to accompany me. Will you come?'

Holmes leaned forward, emptied the Persian slipper into his tobacco pouch and sprang to his feet.

'Give me a moment to pack a clean collar and toothbrush,' he cried. 'I have a spare one for you, Watson. No, my dear fellow, not a word. Where would I be without your assistance? Scribble a note to your wife, and Mrs Hudson will have it delivered. We should be back tomorrow. Now, Gregson, I'm your man and you can fill in the details during our journey.'

The guard's flag was already waving as we rushed up the platform at St Pancras and tore open the door of the first empty smoker. Holmes had brought three travelling-rugs with him and as the train roared its way through the fading winter daylight we made ourselves comfortable enough in our respective corners.

'Well, Gregson, I shall be interested to hear the details,' remarked Holmes, his thin, eager face framed in the ear-flaps of his deer-stalker and a spiral of blue smoke rising from his pipe.

'I know nothing beyond what I have already told you.'

'And yet you used the word "singular" and referred to the telegram from the county police as "curious". Kindly explain.'

'I used both terms for the same reason. The wire from the local inspector advised that the officer from Scotland Yard should read the *Derbyshire County Guide* and the *Gazetteer*. A most extraordinary suggestion!'

'I should say a wise one. What have you done about it?'

'The *Gazetteer* states merely that Lord Jocelyn Cope is a Deputy-Lieutenant and county magnate, married, childless and noted for his bequests to local archaeological societies. As for the *Guide*, I have it here.' He drew a pamphlet from his pocket and thumbed over the pages. 'Here we are,' he continued. 'Arnsworth Castle. Built reign of Edward III. Fifteenth-century stained-glass window to celebrate Battle of Agincourt. Cope family penalised for suspected Catholic leaning by Royal Visitation, 1574. Museum open to public once a year. Contains large collection of martial and other relics including small guillotine built originally in Nîmes during French Revolution for execution of a maternal ancestor of the present owner. Never used owing to escape of intended victim and later purchased as relic by family after Napoleonic

Wars and brought to Arnsworth. Pshaw! That local inspector must be out of his senses, Mr Holmes. There is nothing to help us here.'

'Let us reserve judgement. The man would not have made such a suggestion without reason. In the meantime, I would recommend to your attention the dusk now falling over the landscape. Every material object has become vague and indistinct and yet their solid existence remains, though almost hidden from our visual senses. There is much to be learned from the twilight.'

'Quite so, Mr Holmes,' grinned Gregson, with a wink at me. 'Very poetical, I am sure. Well, I'm for a short nap.'

It was some three hours later that we alighted at a small wayside station. The snow had ceased and beyond the roofs of the hamlet the long desolate slopes of the Derbyshire moors, white and glistening under the light of a full moon, rolled away to the sky-line. A stocky, bow-legged man swathed in a shepherd's plaid hurried towards us along the platform.

'You're from Scotland Yard, I take it?' He greeted us brusquely. 'I got your wire in reply to mine and I have a carriage waiting outside. Yes, I'm Inspector Dawlish,' he added in response to Gregson's question. 'But who are these gentlemen?'

'I considered that Mr Sherlock Holmes's reputation—' began our companion.

'I've never heard of him,' interposed the local man, looking at us with a gleam of hostility in his dark eyes. 'This is a serious affair and there is no room for amateurs. But it is too cold to stand arguing here and, if London approves his presence, who am I to gainsay him? This way, if you please.'

A closed carriage was standing before the station and a moment later we had swung out of the yard and were bowling swiftly but silently up the village high street.

'There'll be accommodation for you at the Queen's Head,' grunted Inspector Dawlish. 'But first to the castle.'

'I shall be glad to hear the facts of this case,' stated Gregson, 'and the reason for the most irregular suggestion contained in your telegram.'

'The facts are simple enough,' replied the other, with a grim smile. 'His lordship has been murdered and we know who did it.'

'Ah!'

'Captain Jasper Lothian, the murdered man's cousin, has disappeared in a hurry. It's common knowledge hereabouts that the man's got a touch of the devil in him, a hard hand with a bottle, a horse or the nearest woman. It's come as a surprise to none of us that Captain Jasper should end by slaughtering his benefactor and the head of his house. Aye, head's a well-chosen word,' he ended softly.

'If you've a clear case, then what's this nonsense about a guide-book?'

Inspector Dawlish leaned forward while his voice sank almost to a whisper. 'You've read it?' he said. 'Then it may interest you to know that Lord Jocelyn Cope was put to death in his own ancestral guillotine.'

His words left us in a chilled silence.

'What motive can you suggest for the murder and for the barbarous method employed?' asked Sherlock Holmes at last.

'Probably a ferocious quarrel. Have I not told you already that Captain Jasper had a touch of the devil in him? But there's the castle, and a proper place it looks for deeds of violence and darkness.'

We had turned off the country road to enter a gloomy avenue that climbed between banked snow-drifts up a barren moorland slope. On the crest loomed a great building, its walls and turrets stark and grey against the night sky. A few minutes later, our carriage rumbled under the arch of the outer bailey and halted in a courtyard.

At Inspector Dawlish's knock, a tall, stooping man in butler's livery opened the massive oaken door and, holding a candle above his head, peered out at us, the light shining on his weary red-rimmed eyes and ill-nourished beard.

'What, four of you!' he cried querulously. 'It b'aint

right her ladyship should be bothered thisways at such a time of grief to us all.'

'That will do, Stephen. Where is her ladyship?'

The candle flame trembled. 'Still with him,' came the reply, and there was something like a sob in the old voice. 'She hasn't moved. Still sitting there in the big chair and staring at him, as though she had fallen fast asleep with them wonderful eyes wide open.'

'You've touched nothing, of course?'

'Nothing. It's all as it was.'

'Then let us go first to the museum where the crime was committed,' said Dawlish. 'It is on the other side of the courtyard.'

He was moving away towards a cleared path that ran across the cobble-stones when Holmes's hand closed upon his arm. 'How is this!' he cried imperiously. 'The museum is on the other side and yet you have allowed a carriage to drive across the courtyard and people to stampede over the ground like a herd of buffalo.'

'What then?'

Holmes flung up his arms appealingly to the moon. 'The snow, man, the snow! You have destroyed your best helpmate.'

'But I tell you the murder was committed in the museum. What has the snow to do with it?'

Holmes gave vent to a most dismal groan and then

we all followed the local detective across the yard to an arched doorway.

I have seen many a grim spectacle during my association with Sherlock Holmes, but I can recall none to surpass in horror the sight that met our eyes within that grey Gothic chamber. It was a small room with a groined roof lit by clusters of tapers in iron sconces. The walls were hung with trophies of armour and mediaeval weapons and edged by glass-topped cases crammed with ancient parchments, thumb-rings, pieces of carved stone-work and yawning man-traps. These details I noticed at a glance and then my whole attention was riveted to the object that occupied a low dais in the centre of the room.

It was a guillotine, painted a faded red and, save for its smaller size, exactly similar to those that I had seen depicted in woodcuts of the French Revolution. Sprawling between the two uprights lay the body of a tall, thin man clad in a velvet smoking-jacket. His hands were tied behind him and a white cloth, hideously besmirched, concealed his head, or rather the place where his head had been.

The light of the tapers, gleaming on a blood-spattered steel blade buried in the lunette, reached beyond to touch as with a halo the red-gold hair of the woman who sat beside that dreadful headless form. Regardless of our approach, she remained motionless in her high carved chair, her features an ivory mask from which two dark and brilliant eyes stared into the shadows with the unwinking fixity of a basilisk. In an experience of women covering three continents, I have never beheld a colder nor a more perfect face than that of the chatelaine of Castle Arnsworth keeping vigil in that chamber of death.

Dawlish coughed.

'You had best retire, my lady,' he said bluntly. 'Rest assured that Inspector Gregson here and I will see that justice is done.'

For the first time, she looked at us, and so uncertain was the light of the tapers that for an instant it seemed to me that some swift emotion more akin to mockery than grief gleamed and died in those wonderful eyes.

'Stephen is not with you?'' she asked incongruously. 'But, of course, he would be in the library. Faithful Stephen.'

'I fear that his lordship's death—'

She rose abruptly, her bosom heaving and one hand gripping the skirt of her black lace gown.

'His damnation!' she hissed, and then, with a gesture of despair, she turned and glided slowly from the room.

As the door closed, Sherlock Holmes dropped on one knee beside the guillotine and, raising the blood-soaked cloth, peered down at the terrible object beneath. 'Dear me,' he said quietly. 'A blow of this force must have sent the head rolling across the room.'

'Probably.'

'I fail to understand. Surely you know where you found it?'

'I didn't find it. There is no head.'

For a long moment, Holmes remained on his knee, staring up silently at the speaker. 'It seems to me that you are taking a great deal for granted,' he said at length, scrambling to his feet. 'Let me hear your ideas on this singular crime.'

'It's plain enough. Sometime last night, the two men quarrelled and eventually came to blows. The younger overpowered the elder and then killed him by means of this instrument. The evidence that Lord Cope was still alive when placed in the guillotine is shown by the fact that Captain Lothian had to lash his hands. The crime was discovered this morning by the butler Stephen, and a groom fetched me from the village whereupon I took the usual steps to identify the body of his lordship and listed the personal belongings found upon him. If you'd like to know how the murderer escaped, I can tell you that too. On the mare that's missing from the stable.'

'Most instructive,' observed Holmes. 'As I understand your theory, the two men engaged in a ferocious combat, being careful not to disarrange any furniture or smash the glass cases that clutter up the room. Then, having disposed of his opponent, the murderer rides into the night, a suitcase under one arm and his victim's head under the other. A truly remarkable performance.'

An angry flush suffused Dawlish's face. 'It's easy enough to pick holes in other people's ideas, Mr Sherlock Holmes,' he sneered. 'Perhaps you will give us your theory.'

'I have none. I am awaiting my facts. By the way, when was your last snowfall?'

'Yesterday afternoon.'

'Then there is hope yet. But let us see if this room will yield us any information.'

For some ten minutes, we stood and watched him, Gregson and I with interest and Dawlish with an ill-concealed look of contempt on his weather-beaten face, as Holmes crawled slowly about the room on his hands and knees muttering and mumbling to himself and looking like some gigantic dun-coloured insect. He had drawn his magnifying-glass from his cape pocket and I noticed that not only the floor but the contents of the occasional tables were subjected to the closest scrutiny. Then, rising to his feet, he stood wrapped in thought, his back to the candlelight and his gaunt shadow falling across the faded red guillotine.

'It won't do,' he said suddenly. 'The murder was premeditated.'

'How do you know?'

'The cranking-handle is freshly oiled, and the victim was senseless. A single jerk would have loosed his hands.'

'Then why were they tied?'

'Ah! There is no doubt, however, that the man was brought here unconscious with his hands already bound.'

'You're wrong there!' interposed Dawlish loudly. 'The design on the lashing proves that it is a sash from one of these window-curtains.'

Holmes shook his head. 'They are faded through exposure to daylight,' said he, 'and this is not. There can be little doubt that it comes from a door-curtain, of which there are none in this room. Well, there is little more to be learned here.'

The two police-agents conferred together and Gregson turned to Holmes. 'As it is after midnight,' said he, 'we had better retire to the village hostelry and tomorrow pursue our enquiries separately. I cannot but agree with Inspector Dawlish that while we are theorising here the murderer may reach the coast.'

'I wish to be clear on one point, Gregson. Am I officially employed on this case by the police?'

'Impossible, Mr Holmes!'

'Quite so. Then I am free to use my own judgement. But give me five minutes in the courtyard and Doctor Watson and I will be with you.'

The bitter cold smote upon us as I slowly followed

the gleam of Holmes's dark lantern along the path that, banked with thick snow, led across the courtyard to the front door. 'Fools!' he cried, stooping over the powdered surface. 'Look at it, Watson! A regiment would have done less damage. Carriage-wheels in three places. And here's Dawlish's boots and a pair of hobnails, probably a groom. A woman now, and running. Of course, Lady Cope and the first alarm. Yes, certainly it is she. What was Stephen doing out here? There is no mistaking his square-toed shoes. Doubtless you observed them, Watson, when he opened the door to us. But what have we here?'

The lantern paused and then moved slowly onwards.

'Pumps. Pumps,' he cried eagerly, 'and coming from the front door. See, here he is again. Probably a tall man, from the size of his feet, and carrying some heavy object. The stride is shortened and the toes more clearly marked than the heels. A burdened man always tends to throw his weight forward. He returns! Ah, just so, just so! Well, I think that we have earned our beds.'

My friend remained silent during our journey back to the village. But, as we separated from Inspector Dawlish at the door of the inn, he laid a hand on his shoulder.

'The man who has done this deed is tall and spare,' said he. 'He is about fifty years of age with a turned-in left foot and strongly addicted to Turkish cigarettes which he smokes from a holder.'

'Captain Lothian!' grunted Dawlish. 'I know nothing about feet or cigarette holders, but the rest of your description is accurate enough. But who told you his appearance?'

'I will set you a question in reply. Were the Copes ever a Catholic family?'

The local inspector glanced significantly at Gregson and tapped his forehead. 'Catholic? Well, now that you mention it, I believe they were in the old times. But what on earth—!'

'Merely that I would recommend you to your own guide-book. Good night.'

On the following morning, after dropping my friend and myself at the castle gate, the two police officers drove off to pursue their enquiries further afield. Holmes watched their departure with a twinkle in his eye.

'I fear that I have done you injustice over the years, Watson,' he commented somewhat enigmatically, as we turned away.

The elderly manservant opened the door to us and, as we followed him into the great hall, it was painfully obvious that the honest fellow was still deeply afflicted by his master's death.

'There is naught for you here,' he cried shrilly. 'My God, will you never leave us in peace?'

I have remarked previously on Holmes's gift for

putting others at their ease, and by degrees the old man recovered his composure. 'I take it that this is the Agincourt window,' observed Holmes, staring up at a small but exquisitely coloured stained-glass casement through which the winter sunlight threw a pattern of brilliant colours on the ancient stone floor.

'It is, sir. Only two in all England.'

'Doubtless you have served the family for many years,' continued my friend gently.

'Served 'em? Aye, me and mine for nigh two centuries. Ours is the dust that lies upon their funeral palls.'

'I fancy they have an interesting history.'

'They have that, sir.'

'I seem to have heard that this ill-omened guillotine was specially built for some ancestor of your late master?'

'Aye, the Marquis de Rennes. Built by his own tenants, the varmints, hated him, they did, simply because he kept up old customs.'

'Indeed. What custom?'

'Something about women, sir. The book in the library don't explain exactly.'

'*Le droit du seigneur,* perhaps.'

'Well, I don't speak heathern, but I believe them was the very words.'

'H'm. I should like to see this library.'

The old man's eyes slid to a door at the end of the hall.

'See the library?' he grumbled. 'What do you want there? Nothing but old books, and her ladyship don't like—Oh, very well.'

He led the way ungraciously into a long, low room lined to the ceiling with volumes and ending in a magnificent Gothic fireplace. Holmes, after strolling about listlessly, paused to light a cheroot.

'Well, Watson, I think that we'll be getting back,' said he. 'Thank you, Stephen. It is a fine room, though I am surprised to see Indian rugs.'

'Indian!' protested the old man indignantly. 'They're antique Persian.'

'Surely Indian.'

'Persian, I tell you! Them marks are inscriptions, as a gentleman like you should know. Can't see without your spy-glass? Well, use it then. Now, drat it, if he hasn't spilled his matches!'

As we rose to our feet after gathering up the scattered vestas, I was puzzled to account for the sudden flush of excitement in Holmes's sallow cheeks.

'I was mistaken,' said he. 'They are Persian. Come, Watson, it is high time that we set out for the village and our train back to town.'

A few minutes later, we had left the castle. But to my surprise, on emerging from the outer bailey, Holmes led the way swiftly along a lane leading to the stables.

'You intend to enquire about the missing horse,' I suggested.

'The horse? My dear fellow, I have no doubt that it is safely concealed in one of the home farms, while Gregson rushes all over the county. This is what I am looking for.'

He entered the first loose box and returned with his arms full of straw. 'Another bundle for you, Watson, and it should be enough for our purpose.'

'But what is our purpose?'

'Principally to reach the front door without being observed,' he chuckled, as he shouldered his burden. Having retraced our footsteps, Holmes laid his finger on his lips and, cautiously opening the great door, slipped into a nearby closet, full of capes and sticks, where he proceeded to throw both our bundles on the floor.

'It should be safe enough,' he whispered, 'for it is stone-built. Ah! These two mackintoshes will assist admirably. I have no doubt,' he added, as he struck a match and dropped it into the pile, 'that I shall have other occasions to use this modest stratagem.'

As the flames spread through the straw and reached the mackintoshes, thick black wreaths of smoke poured from the cloak-room door into the hall of Arnsworth Castle, accompanied by a hissing and crackling from the burning rubber.

'Good heavens, Holmes,' I gasped, the tears rolling down my face. 'We shall be suffocated!'

His fingers closed on my arm.

'Wait,' he muttered, and even as he spoke, there came a sudden rush of feet and a yell of horror.

'Fire!'

In that despairing wail, I recognised Stephen's voice. 'Fire!' he shrieked again, and we caught the clatter of his footsteps as he fled across the hall.

'Now!' whispered Holmes and, in an instant, he was out of the cloak-room and running headlong for the library. The door was half open but, as we burst in, the man drumming with hysterical hands on the great fireplace did not even turn his head.

'Fire! The house is on fire!' he shrieked. 'Oh, my poor master! My lord! My lord!'

Holmes's hand fell upon his shoulder. 'A bucket of water in the cloak-room will meet the case,' he said quietly. 'It would be as well, however, if you would ask his lordship to join us.'

The old man sprang at him, his eyes blazing and his fingers crooked like the talons of a vulture.

'A trick!' he screamed. 'I've betrayed him through your cursed tricks!'

'Take him, Watson,' said Holmes, holding him at arm's length. 'There, there. You're a faithful fellow.'

'Faithful unto death,' whispered a feeble voice.

I started back involuntarily. The edge of the ancient

fireplace had swung open and in the dark aperture thus disclosed there stood a tall, thin man, so powdered with dust that for the moment I seemed to be staring not at a human being but at a spectre. He was about fifty years of age, gaunt and high-nosed, with a pair of sombre eyes that waxed and waned feverishly in a face that was the colour of grey paper.

'I fear that the dust is bothering you, Lord Cope,' said Holmes very gently. 'Would you not be better seated?'

The man tottered forward to drop heavily into an armchair. 'You are the police, of course,' he gasped.

'No. I am a private investigator, but acting in the interests of justice.'

A bitter smile parted Lord Cope's lips.

'Too late,' said he.

'You are ill?'

'I am dying.' Opening his fingers, he disclosed a small empty phial. 'There is only a short time left to me.'

'Is there nothing to be done, Watson?'

I laid my fingers upon the sick man's wrist. His face was already livid and the pulse slow and feeble.

'Nothing, Holmes.'

Lord Cope straightened himself painfully. 'Perhaps you will indulge a last curiosity by telling me how you discovered the truth,' said he. 'You must be a man of some perception.'

'I confess that at first there were difficulties,' admitted Holmes, 'though these dissolved themselves later in the light of events. Obviously the whole key to the problem lay in a conjunction of two remarkable circumstances – the use of a guillotine and the disappearance of the murdered man's head.

'Who, I asked myself, would use so clumsy and rare an instrument, except one to whom it possessed some strong symbolic significance and, if this were the case, then it was logical to suppose that the clue to that significance must lie in its past history.'

The nobleman nodded.

'His own people built it for Rennes,' he muttered, 'in return for the infamy that their womenfolk had suffered at his hands. But pray proceed, and quickly.'

'So much for the first circumstance,' continued Holmes, ticking off the points on his fingers. 'The second threw a flood of light over the whole problem. This is not New Guinea. Why, then, should a murderer take his victim's head? The obvious answer was that he wished to conceal the dead man's true identity. By the way,' he demanded sternly, 'what have you done with Captain Lothian's head?'

'Stephen and I buried it at midnight in the family vault,' came the feeble reply. 'And that with all reverence.'

'The rest was simple,' went on Holmes. 'As the body

was easily identifiable as yours by the clothes and other personal belongings which were listed by the local inspector, it followed naturally that there could have been no point in concealing the head unless the murderer had also changed clothes with the dead man. That the change had been effected before death was shown by the blood-stains. The victim had been incapacitated in advance, probably drugged, for it was plain from certain facts already explained to my friend Watson that there had been no struggle and that he had been carried to the museum from another part of the castle. Assuming my reasoning to be correct, then the murdered man could not be Lord Jocelyn. But was there not another missing, his lordship's cousin and alleged murderer, Captain Jasper Lothian?'

'How could you give Dawlish a description of the wanted man?' I interposed.

'By looking at the body of the victim, Watson. The two men must have borne a general resemblance to each other or the deception would not have been feasible from the start. An ash tray in the museum contained a cigarette stub, Turkish, comparatively fresh and smoked from a holder. None but an addict would have smoked under the terrible circumstances that must have accompanied that insignificant stump. The footmarks in the snow showed that someone had come from the main building carrying a burden and had returned without that burden. I think I have covered the principal points.'

For a while, we sat in silence broken only by the moan of a rising wind at the windows and the short, sharp panting of the dying man's breath.

'I owe you no explanation,' he said at last, 'for it is to my Maker, who alone knows the innermost recesses of the human heart, that I must answer for my deed. Nevertheless, though my story is one of shame and guilt, I shall tell you enough to enlist perhaps your forbearance in granting me my final request.

'You must know, then, that following the scandal which brought his Army career to its close, my cousin Jasper Lothian has lived at Arnsworth. Though penniless and already notorious for his evil living, I welcomed him as a kinsman, affording him not only financial support but, what was perhaps more valuable, the social aegis of my position in the county.

'As I look back now on the years that passed, I blame myself for my own lack of principle in my failure to put an end to his extravagance, his drinking and gaming, and certain less honourable pursuits with which rumour already linked his name. I had thought him wild and injudicious. I was yet to learn that he was a creature so vile and utterly bereft of honour that he would tarnish the name of his own house.

'I had married a woman considerably younger than myself, a woman as remarkable for her beauty as for her romantic yet singular temperament which she had inherited from her Spanish forebears. It was the old story, and when at long last I awoke to the dreadful truth it was also to the knowledge that only one thing remained for me in life – vengeance. Vengeance against this man who had disgraced my name and abused the honour of my house.

'On the night in question, Lothian and I sat late over our wine in this very room. I had contrived to drug his port and before the effects of the narcotic could deaden his senses I told him of my discovery and that death alone could wipe out the score. He sneered back at me that in killing him I would merely put myself on the scaffold and expose my wife's shame to the world. When I explained my plan, the sneer was gone from his face and the terror of death was freezing in his black heart. The rest you know. As the drug deprived him of his senses, I changed clothes with him, bound his hands with a sash torn from the door-curtain and carried him across the courtyard to the museum, to the virgin guillotine which had been built for another's infamy.

'When it was over, I summoned Stephen and told him the truth. The old man never hesitated in his loyalty to his wretched master. Together we buried the head in the family vault and then, seizing a mare from the stable, he rode it across the moor to convey an impression of flight and finally left it concealed in a lonely farm owned by his sister. All that remained was for me to disappear.

'Arnsworth, like many mansions belonging to families that had been Catholic in the olden times, possessed a priest's hole. There I have lain concealed, emerging only at night into the library to lay my final instructions upon my faithful servant.'

'Thereby confirming my suspicion as to your proximity,' interposed Holmes, 'by leaving no fewer than five smears of Turkish tobacco ash upon the rugs. But what was your ultimate intention?'

'In taking vengeance for the greatest wrong which one man can do to another, I had successfully protected our name from the shame of the scaffold. I could rely on Stephen's loyalty. As for my wife, though she knew the truth she could not betray me without announcing to the world her own infidelity. Life held nothing more for me. I determined therefore to allow myself a day or two in which to get my affairs in order and then to die by my own hand. I assure you that your discovery of my hiding-place has advanced the event by only an hour or so. I had left a letter for Stephen, begging him as his final devoir that he would bury my body secretly in the vaults of my ancestors.

'There, gentlemen, is my story. I am the last of the old

line and it lies with you whether or not it shall go out in dishonour.'

Sherlock Holmes laid a hand upon his.

'It is perhaps as well that it has been pointed out to us already that my friend Watson and I are here in an entirely private capacity,' said he quietly. 'I am about to summon Stephen, for I cannot help feeling that you would be more comfortable if he carried this chair into the priest's hole and closed the sliding panel after you.'

We had to bend our heads to catch Lord Jocelyn's response.

'Then a higher tribunal will judge my crime,' he whispered faintly, 'and the tomb shall devour my secret. Farewell, and may a dying man's blessing rest upon you.'

Our journey back to London was both chilly and depressing. With nightfall, the snow had recommenced and Holmes was in his least communicative mood, staring out of the window at the scattered lights of villages and farm-houses that periodically flitted past in the darkness.

'The old year is nodding to its fall,' he remarked suddenly, 'and in the hearts of all these kindly, simple folk awaiting the midnight chimes dwells the perennial anticipation that what is to come will be better than what has been. Hope, however ingenuous and disproven by past experience, remains the one supreme panacea for all the knocks and bruises which life metes out to us.' He leaned back and began to stuff his pipe with shag.

'Should you eventually write an account of this curious affair in Derbyshire,' he went on, 'I would suggest that a suitable title would be "The Red Widow".'

'Knowing your unreasonable aversion to women, Holmes, I am surprised that you noticed the colour of her hair.'

'I refer, Watson, to the popular sobriquet for a guillotine in the days of the French Revolution,' he said severely.

The hour was late when, at last, we reached our old lodgings in Baker Street where Holmes, after poking up the fire, lost not a moment in donning his mouse-coloured dressing-gown.

'It is approaching midnight,' I observed, 'and as I would wish to be with my wife when this year of 1887 draws to its close, I must be on my way. Let me wish you a happy New Year, my dear fellow.'

'I heartily reciprocate your good wishes, Watson,' he replied. 'Pray bear my greetings to your wife and my apologies for your temporary absence.'

I had reached the deserted street and, pausing for a moment to raise my collar against the swirl of the snow-flakes, I was about to set out on my walk when my attention was arrested by the strains of a violin. Involuntarily, I raised my eyes to the window of our old sitting-room and there, sharply outlined against the lamplit blind, was the shadow of Sherlock Holmes. I could see that keen, hawk-like profile which I knew so well, the slight stoop of his shoulders as he bent over his fiddle, the rise and fall of the bow-tip. But surely this was no dreamy Italian air, no complicated improvisation of his own creation, that drifted down to me through the stillness of that bleak winter's night.

Should auld acquaintance be forgot
And never brought to mind'?
Should auld acquaintance be forgot
And days o' auld lang syne.

A snowflake must have drifted into my eyes for, as I turned away, the gas-lamps glimmering down the desolate expanse of Baker Street seemed strangely blurred.

* * *

My task is done. My notebooks have been replaced in the black tin deed-box where they have been kept in recent years and, for the last time, I have dipped my pen in the ink-well.

Through the window that overlooks the modest lawn of our farm-house, I can see Sherlock Holmes strolling among his beehives. His hair is quite white, but his long, thin form is as wiry and energetic as ever, and there is a touch of healthy colour in his cheeks, placed there by Mother Nature and her clover-laden breezes that carry the scent of the sea amid these gentle Sussex Downs.

Our lives are drawing towards eventide and old faces and old scenes are gone for ever. And yet, as I lean back in my chair and close my eyes, for a while the past rises up to obscure the present and I see before me the yellow fogs of Baker Street and I hear once more the voice of the best and wisest man whom I have ever known. 'Come, Watson, the game's afoot!'

In the case of the Darlington Substitution Scandal
it was of use to me, and also in
the Arnsworth Castle business.

FROM 'A SCANDAL IN BOHEMIA'

Camberwell Crackers

Anthony Horowitz

'I'll try not to take up too much of your time, Mr Fulbright,' the detective said. 'But I'd be interested to know what you can tell me about the dead man.'

'Well, not very much, Detective Inspector. I only ever met him once.'

'He came here.'

'That's right. He paid us a visit … I suppose it must have been four or five weeks ago. He didn't stay very long. I showed him round the factory and then he had a cup of tea, here in this office.'

'What did you make of him?'

'I don't quite know how to answer that. He was quite brusque but then of course he was a businessman and it

68

was business that had brought him here. He struck me as someone who didn't like to waste time.'

'Were you surprised to hear that he had been killed?'

'I was shocked. We all were. Did you notice the wreath in the reception area? One of the lads brought it in. A very nice gesture, I thought.'

Reception area … wreath. Andrew Fletcher jotted the words down in his notebook and underlined them – not because they were important but because he felt a need to look as if he was in control.

He wasn't.

This was the first murder he had investigated since he had become a Detective Inspector at the unusually young age of twenty-seven. There had been a lot of bad-mouthing back at the station but the moment he had heard about the death of multi-millionaire, Harvey Osborne, he had known that this was his chance to prove himself. Yes, he had been privately educated. And yes, he was lucky enough to have been fast-tracked for promotion. But he was going to show them! He wasn't the chinless wonder they all believed – and having an uncle who happened to be Assistant Commissioner was also completely irrelevant.

The trouble was, as far as he could see nothing made sense. The murder itself was completely crazy and he had already decided that coming here was a complete waste of time.

It was frankly hard to believe that somewhere like Fulbright's Christmas Cracker Factory – or Camberwell Crackers as it was fondly known to all the locals – could exist in London in the twenty-first century. It was housed in a neat, Victorian building just off Denmark Hill, complete with red bricks, sash windows and a chimney which had given up smoking, surrounded by lawns and ornate metalwork, a world of its own. The reception area boasted wood panelling, a swirly carpet and a demure receptionist straight out of World War Two. Sure enough, there had been a funeral wreath of white roses and lilies, resting on an easel. There had even been a book of condolences although Fletcher had noticed the pages were all blank.

'Mr Fulbright? Yes, certainly. I'll just call him.' The receptionist somehow managed to smile and look severe at the same time. She had been knitting when the detective came in. Did anyone still knit? Perhaps she had a sister or a friend who was expecting a child.

The factory supervisor – and indeed its owner – had appeared a few minutes later: a small, neat, bald-headed man in a dark suit and brightly polished shoes. He had a moustache which, though not quite so extreme, reminded Fletcher of that annoying man, the opera singer who had once appeared in insurance commercials. He was about sixty years old, twitching and apologising before he had even shaken hands.

'So sorry to keep you ... a busy time for us ... Christmas only just round the corner ... of course you understand.'

The words came tumbling out. He was obviously nervous about something but Fletcher's first impression was that he would make an unlikely murder suspect. Arthur Fulbright was the sort of man who would only meet a police officer if he was stopped for speeding and even then it would only be five or six miles per hour over the limit. He had a sort of twitchy nervousness which came from not wanting to get into trouble. He was probably married to a wife who nagged him. Fletcher could imagine him walking three paces behind her, carrying the shopping.

They did not go straight to the office. Fulbright insisted on showing the detective around the factory, introducing him to everyone who worked there. In all, there were about twenty of them spread across the different departments: novelties (purchasing and assembly), tube construction, wrapping design, packaging, marketing, distribution and sales. The manufacturing floor was semi-automated in a Heath Robinson sort of way with tubes of cardboard and brightly coloured foil at one end, the finished boxes stacking up at the other. The workers were old and young, male and female, from every ethnic background and seemed absurdly cheerful, as if the spirit of Christmas infused the place the whole year round.

'This is Rita Patel who does our accounts.' Fulbright beamed at a tiny woman perched on a stool, then moved towards a plump man in a brightly checked V-neck sweater who was sitting at a desk with a fountain pen and ink all over his fingers. 'And this is Mr Thompson. He is a very important part of our operation. Mr Thompson writes our jokes.'

'Delighted!' Mr Thompson exclaimed.

'This is Detective Inspector Fletcher. I wonder if you have a joke for him?'

Mr Thompson laid down his pen. 'Who hides in a bakery at Christmas?' he asked, and before Fletcher could answer, replied, 'A mince spy. What's white and goes up? A confused snowflake. What bird is out of breath? A puffin. What's the fastest thing on a river …?'

'Thank you, Mr Thompson!' The two of them hurried on. 'A brilliant mind,' Fulbright confided. 'He's been with us for twenty years. He once worked with Ben Elton. And here's the complete range …'

The crackers lay stacked out in front of them. There were traditional crackers, modern crackers, luxury crackers, themed crackers – all stamped with the Camberwell logo and snuggling together in packets of twelve. Two youths in loose-fitting brown coats, barely out of their teens, were arranging the boxes. Like everyone else in the factory, they seemed absurdly pleased to be here.

'This is Walter. And this is Jomo. When I started here, they would have been called apprentices. Now I have to call them interns. But it's the same principle. We like to support local youth … no zero-hour contracts or anything like that! I'd like to think that these two have a bright future. Jomo is already an accomplished plastic holly engineer and we've got Walter working on seasonal mottoes. Have you seen enough, Detective Inspector? Shall we go upstairs?'

Thirty minutes later, after a homely woman had served them tea and chocolate digestive biscuits, the two men were sitting in a comfortable office, facing each other across a leather-topped desk. Fulbright owned a laptop computer, Fletcher noticed. But he kept it closed, almost as if he was ashamed of it.

'I have to say, I'm a little surprised you've come here,' Fulbright said. 'I hope you don't think that anybody at Camberwell Crackers would have had anything to do with Mr Osborne's death.'

'Not at all, sir. It's simply police procedure. We have to talk to everybody who met Mr Osborne in the weeks before he died.'

'Well, as I told you, he certainly did come here.'

'He was a shareholder, I understand.'

'Yes. In fact, he had acquired a majority shareholding in the company.'

'Fifty-one per cent.'

'Fifty-five, I believe.'

'Did Mr Osborne have any plans for Camberwell Crackers?'

'Absolutely. He was very helpful. He wanted us to consider investing in new plant and he had some interesting suggestions about our range.'

'What sort of ideas?'

'Oh – bigger crackers. Firework crackers ... although I had to explain to him that indoor fireworks are no longer viable because of EU regulations. Luxury crackers! That was an interesting thought. Crackers with gold or silver bangles inside them. Of course, this was only a preliminary meeting but I must say, I was quite excited by his vision. He was a man who clearly didn't have the faintest idea what he was talking about but at the same time he was most definitely prepared to learn. He wanted to know everything about the business. We arranged to meet again in the New Year and I was extremely sorry to hear of his demise.' Fulbright paused, touching a discreet finger to his chin. 'Do you have any suspects?'

'Not as yet, sir.'

Fletcher wished he could answer differently. It had been almost a month since the murder now and already they were sniggering at the office and one or two very hurtful messages had been chalked up on the incidents board. He had done everything by the book. He had interviewed Osborne's two ex-wives, his various sons, the business partners, the new girlfriend, the servants and the neighbours and there was at least one thing that he had quickly learned. They all, in varying degrees, disliked the dead man. It was actually quite remarkable how many of them might have wanted to kill him. In fact, Arthur Fulbright was the only person he'd met who had anything good to say about him.

And yet the whole lot of them had alibis. None of them could have committed the crime and, with mounting frustration, Fletcher had been forced to eliminate each one of them from his enquiries. Worse still, even if they had been unable to account for their whereabouts, there was something about the nature of the crime, the way it had been committed that didn't seem to fit any of them.

He glanced down at the almost empty page of his notebook, vaguely trying to remember what he had been taught at police training school. He had no idea what to ask next. 'You are aware that Mr Osborne had a reputation as an asset-stripper,' he said, at length.

'I'm quite surprised to hear it.' The factory owner took a bite of his digestive biscuit. His teeth left a perfect half-circle, like an eclipse. 'Maybe he would have revealed himself in due course. But as I've said, he seemed completely enthusiastic. Camberwell Crackers are a very well-known brand and he made it quite clear that he was delighted to have acquired us as part of his business portfolio.'

'Delighted?'

'That was what he said.'

* * *

Arthur Fulbright was lying.

It hadn't been like that at all.

A month before, Harvey Osborne had arrived at the factory in his chauffeur-driven, midnight blue, Mercedes S-Class saloon and had marched in as if he owned the place which, he had quickly made clear, he did. In his sports jacket, Tattersall shirt and flat cap, he looked more like a country squire than a businessman. Tilda, on the reception, had got things off to a bad start by asking him if he was applying for a job in the factory canteen. Osborne, who had been educated at Eton, had smiled at her with eyes that announced her death sentence. He had simply told her to call the manager.

Tilda had telephoned the office and Arthur Fulbright had come down to the reception area, just as he had for Detective Inspector Fletcher. He made a habit of never sending his secretary. He thought it was discourteous. But from the moment of their meeting, everything had been difficult. Osborne was about twenty years younger than the factory manager but success in business and wealth had given him a natural superiority. He had grey skin, close-cropped hair and exceptionally hard eyes. He did not offer to shake hands. In fact, he was wearing leather gloves which he never removed.

'You're Fulbright? Let's get on with it, shall we? You know who I am?'

'Of course.'

'OK. Let's take a quick look round and then we can get down to brass tacks.'

Osborne had shown no enthusiasm as he was shown around the factory and had refused to greet anyone on first-name or indeed on any-name terms. He hadn't even tried to smile at Mr Thompson's jokes and had surveyed the product lines with ill-concealed disdain. Once they had reached the privacy of Fulbright's office, he had come straight to the point.

'I'm shutting you down.'

Mr Fulbright had blinked and laid his biscuit – this time a Jammie Dodger – back on its plate. 'I'm sorry?'

'This business doesn't make any sense. What's a Christmas cracker factory doing in the middle of Camberwell?'

'It was founded by my great-grandfather.'

'I don't think you're quite getting my drift, Fulbright. I don't care if your family has been here since the middle ages. This building is a waste of space.'

'We're highly profitable.'

'You're just about breaking even. But the fact is, if this site was redeveloped – houses, offices, retail outlets – it would be worth millions. I'm amazed you never saw it. We're in south London for Christ's sake! You could be making your product anywhere. Why do you want to make it here?'

'We've always been very much part of the local community.'

'Oh per-lease!' Osborne held up a gloved hand. 'Don't start talking to me about community and social cohesion and all that crap. I'm only interested in business. And take it from me, mate, this business makes no sense.'

'People like Christmas crackers …'

'They only like them at Christmas and that's once a year! Hardly a brilliant start for a business model. Anyway, they can buy them from China and Eastern Europe at half the price.'

'We pride ourselves on our quality.'

'Quality?' The businessman threw back his head and laughed. 'You're not making Swiss watches here. You're not making integrated circuits. Shall I tell you something? Speaking personally, I don't give a damn about Christmas. Next December … I'll be on my yacht in the Caribbean, as far away from it as I can get. I hate Christmas trees, Christmas carols, Christmas lights and all the rest of it.

Stupid Christmas cards with robins and three wise men. Bloody pantomimes at the theatre and people queuing up to buy stuff they don't want and which will be in the bin before January.

'But shall I tell you what I hate most about Christmas? Christmas crackers! Even when I was a kid I never understood them. I mean, first of all they look stupid and then you rip them apart. And there's nothing inside! All you get is a crap novelty – one hundred per cent useless. Has anybody ever got anything decent out of a cracker? The crap novelty, the stupid hat, the joke that isn't funny. Useless! Useless! Useless! Why do you even bother?'

Arthur Fulbright had listened to all this in silence but two red pin-pricks had appeared in his cheeks and for once the polite smile had vanished from his lips. He had no understanding of finance. He didn't know how this man had acquired the shares. All he wanted was for the interview to be over. 'If I understand you correctly,' he said, 'you want us to move.'

'Here's my problem,' Osborne returned. 'I could move you. We could fire the staff and hire a new workforce somewhere cheaper. Somewhere up in the north ...'

'I wouldn't wish to fire my staff,' Fulbright interrupted.

'That's exactly my point. If I was doing the firing, you'd be the first to go. I knew it the moment I walked in here. This is a family business. Duh! You know a lot about family but nothing about business and that's why you're not making money. It doesn't matter where I put you, Mr Fulbright. North, south, east or west, you're not going to make a sensible profit. So you know what? It's easier just to close you down.'

* * *

That was how it had really gone. But of course Arthur Fulbright couldn't tell the detective that. He didn't know a great deal about police methods but he had watched enough Poirot and Morse on television to realise how very easily he could make himself the prime suspect in the businessman's murder.

'How long did Mr Osborne stay here?' the detective asked.

'About an hour. He asked a lot of quite penetrating questions about the Christmas cracker business and he was very keen – dead keen I would say, although perhaps that isn't appropriate in the circumstances – to learn more.'

'How did he leave it?'

'As I said, we arranged to meet again in January.' Fulbright shook his head, downcast. 'He talked about re-investment. I'd hate to think that his untimely death would put an end to that.'

'I can't tell you that.'

'He didn't talk to anyone else about his visit here?'

Fletcher shook his head. 'Unfortunately not. Mr Osborne seems to have been something of a one-man band in the way he operated and he'd fired his secretary the month before he died so she couldn't tell us anything. I've looked through his diary and computer files but frankly it's all a mess.'

'Oh dear. That's most unsatisfactory. I suppose that when the dust settles we'll just have to continue as we have always done – without any help from outside.'

There was nothing more to be said. DI Martin Fletcher folded his notebook with the bitter knowledge that he was no closer to the truth. Perhaps, he reflected, it was the ex-secretary after all. Osborne had fired her for no reason and without references and she was spitting blood. But then again, what about the mistress? It was clear that Osborne had been brutal to her. And then there was the business partner who had just come out of jail ...

'Thank you for your time, sir,' he said.

'You have no more questions, Detective Inspector?'

'Not at this stage. No.'

'Let me show you out.'

The two men stood up and left together.

'So how exactly did Mr Osborne die?' Fulbright asked as they made their way out of the office. He posed the question quite casually, as if merely to make conversation rather than because he really wanted to know.

DI Fletcher thought back to the photographs and files that littered his desk. It was amazing how much police work still relied on paper.

Harvey Osborne had lived in a huge house in Richmond with one hundred metres' private frontage onto the River Thames. The house was modern but built in the Regency style with a swimming pool in the basement, a cinema suite, a snooker room, and a kitchen that could have supported a three-star London restaurant. He lived there alone. His second wife had been kicked out and his mistress had a two-bedroom flat in Fulham. On the night of the murder, Osborne had been asleep in his luxurious bedroom on the first floor. He must have thought he was safe. The house was completely surrounded by a fifteen-metre wall with CCTV everywhere. An electrically operated gate provided the only way in and it was guarded by a cabin with three Estonian security men on twenty-four-hour standby.

It should have been impossible to break in.

'I'll tell you what we know,' Fletcher said. 'Although of course this is highly confidential.'

'I understand.'

Fletcher had decided to run through it one more time with Arthur Fulbright, even though he knew he shouldn't. But he had the vague hope that spelling it all out, going over it step by step might help him to see it all more clearly and perhaps to spot the single clue he was sure he was missing.

'It happened at midnight on November 10th. That was just over three weeks ago. Mr Osborne was alone in the house but his security detail – three men – were in the cabin by the front gate. And this is where it starts. They should have been patrolling the grounds but they weren't. It seems that a few days before, somebody had sent them a set of plastic poker dice. You know Estonians love to gamble. Well, they were totally absorbed in the game and that was why they didn't step outside.

'The intruder – let's assume he was a man – arrived at midnight and the first thing he did was to lock the security men into the cabin, using a miniature padlock which he fixed to a hasp on the door. Even if they'd broken off from their game, it would hold them up when they tried to get out.

'Then the killer set to work on the front gate. There was an electronic keypad which controlled it but he unscrewed that with a miniature screwdriver and then set to work on the wires. They were tightly packed together and according to forensics, he used a device not dissimilar to a nail clipper to cut through them. He connected two of the wires with a stapler which he must have brought with him and that caused a short-circuit which opened the gate.

'The garden was pitch black and he couldn't risk being seen but we think he used a very small torch and possibly a compass to navigate his way forward. When he reached the front door, he picked the lock with a pair of tweezers and that was how he got into the hall. Osborne had an infra-red beam in front of the stairs which would have set off the alarms but our guy was smart. He had brought powder compacts – the sort young girls use for make-up – and he positioned them very carefully, using a tape measure. They refracted the beam and he was able to continue up the stairs and into Osborne's bedroom.'

'Did he have a gun?'

'No. The murder weapon was particularly horrible. He used a length of paper which he had soaked in silver oxidoazaniumylidynemethane – an extremely unstable chemical also known as silver fulminate. It is a primary explosive, highly sensitive to friction. The intruder looped the paper around Mr Osborne's neck and then tightened it. The result was an explosion which blew Mr Osborne's head off.'

'How dreadful, Detective Inspector. But you mentioned CCTV. Surely they will have photographed the man.'

'The man or the woman! Oh yes, sir. We have images

of him all right. But unfortunately he was wearing a brightly coloured tissue mask around his face with holes cut out for his eyes. There is absolutely no way we can identify him.'

'And he got away?'

'The guards realised something was wrong when they heard the explosion and managed to break out of the cabin. But the killer had strewn marbles along the path and all three of them were thrown off their feet. This gave him enough time to make his escape – not back to the main road – but down the river. We're not yet sure what sort of vessel he used but it was certainly fast because he was gone before the guards got anywhere near.'

'The fastest thing on a river? I would suspect that would be a motor-pike.'

'I'm sorry, sir?'

It seemed to Fletcher that a smile had flickered across the face of Arthur Fulbright which had quite changed his appearance. For just a few seconds he had looked quite cruel. But the smile had already gone and Fletcher was sure he had imagined it.

'Nothing, Detective Inspector.'

'Well, anyway, sir, that's how it was. And now if you'll excuse me …'

Fletcher got up. The two men shook hands and he made his way back downstairs. He had definitely decided he would interview the secretary again. The more he thought about it, the more suspicious she seemed.

Tilda, the receptionist, gave him a box of Camberwell Crackers on the way out. It was a very nice thought. 'Happy Christmas,' she said.

'Happy Christmas,' Fletcher replied and stepped out into the gently falling snow.

The Flying Stars

G. K. Chesterton

'The most beautiful crime I ever committed,' Flambeau would say in his highly moral old age, 'was also, by a singular coincidence, my last. It was committed at Christmas. As an artist I had always attempted to provide crimes suitable to the special season or landscapes in which I found myself, choosing this or that terrace or garden for a catastrophe, as if for a statuary group. Thus squires should be swindled in long rooms panelled with oak; while Jews, on the other hand, should rather find themselves unexpectedly penniless among the lights and screens of the Cafe Riche. Thus, in England, if I wished to relieve a dean of his riches (which is not so easy as you might suppose), I wished to frame him, if I make myself clear, in the green lawns and grey towers of some cathedral town. Similarly, in France, when I had got money out of a rich and wicked peasant (which is almost impossible), it gratified me to get his indignant head relieved against a grey line of clipped poplars, and those solemn plains of Gaul over which broods the mighty spirit of Millet.

'Well, my last crime was a Christmas crime, a cheery, cosy, English middle-class crime; a crime of Charles Dickens. I did it in a good old middle-class house near Putney, a house with a crescent of carriage drive, a house with a stable by the side of it, a house with the name on the two outer gates, a house with a monkey tree. Enough, you know the species. I really think my imitation of Dickens's style was dexterous and literary. It seems almost a pity I repented the same evening.'

Flambeau would then proceed to tell the story from the inside; and even from the inside it was odd. Seen from the outside it was perfectly incomprehensible, and it is from the outside that the stranger must study it. From this standpoint the drama may be said to have begun when the front doors of the house with the stable opened on the garden with the monkey tree, and a young girl came out with bread to feed the birds on the afternoon of Boxing Day. She had a pretty face, with brave brown eyes; but her figure was beyond conjecture, for she was so wrapped up in brown furs that it was hard to say which was hair and which was fur. But for the attractive face she might have been a small toddling bear.

The winter afternoon was reddening towards evening, and already a ruby light was rolled over the bloomless beds, filling them, as it were, with the ghosts of the dead roses. On one side of the house stood the stable, on the other an alley or cloister of laurels led to the larger garden behind. The young lady, having scattered bread for the birds (for the fourth or fifth time that day, because the dog ate it), passed unobtrusively down the lane of laurels and into a glimmering plantation of evergreens behind. Here she gave an exclamation of wonder, real or ritual, and looking up at the high garden wall above her, beheld it fantastically bestridden by a somewhat fantastic figure.

'Oh, don't jump, Mr Crook,' she called out in some alarm; 'it's much too high.'

The individual riding the party wall like an aerial horse was a tall, angular young man, with dark hair sticking up like a hair brush, intelligent and even distinguished lineaments, but a sallow and almost alien complexion. This showed the more plainly because he wore an aggressive red tie, the only part of his costume of which he seemed to take any care. Perhaps it was a symbol. He took no notice of the girl's alarmed adjuration, but leapt like a grasshopper to the ground beside her, where he might very well have broken his legs.

'I think I was meant to be a burglar,' he said placidly, 'and I have no doubt I should have been if I hadn't happened to be born in that nice house next door. I can't see any harm in it, anyhow.'

'How can you say such things!' she remonstrated.

'Well,' said the young man, 'if you're born on the wrong side of the wall, I can't see that it's wrong to climb over it.'

'I never know what you will say or do next,' she said.

'I don't often know myself,' replied Mr Crook; 'but then I am on the right side of the wall now.'

'And which is the right side of the wall?' asked the young lady, smiling.

'Whichever side you are on,' said the young man named Crook.

As they went together through the laurels towards the front garden a motor horn sounded thrice, coming nearer and nearer, and a car of splendid speed, great elegance, and a pale green colour swept up to the front doors like a bird and stood throbbing.

'Hullo, hullo!' said the young man with the red tie, 'here's somebody born on the right side, anyhow. I didn't know, Miss Adams, that your Santa Claus was so modern as this.'

'Oh, that's my godfather, Sir Leopold Fischer. He always comes on Boxing Day.'

Then, after an innocent pause, which unconsciously betrayed some lack of enthusiasm, Ruby Adams added:

'He is very kind.'

John Crook, journalist, had heard of that eminent City magnate; and it was not his fault if the City magnate had not heard of him; for in certain articles in *The Clarion* or *The New Age* Sir Leopold had been dealt with austerely. But he said nothing and grimly watched the unloading of the motor-car, which was rather a long process. A large, neat chauffeur in green got out from the front, and a small, neat manservant in grey got out from the back, and between them they deposited Sir Leopold on the doorstep and began to unpack him, like some very carefully protected parcel. Rugs enough to stock a bazaar, furs of all the beasts of the forest, and scarves of all the colours of the rainbow were unwrapped one by one, till they revealed something resembling the human form; the form of a friendly, but foreign-looking old gentleman, with a grey goat-like beard and a beaming smile, who rubbed his big fur gloves together.

Long before this revelation was complete the two big doors of the porch had opened in the middle, and Colonel Adams (father of the furry young lady) had come out himself to invite his eminent guest inside. He was a tall, sunburnt, and very silent man, who wore a red smoking-cap like a fez, making him look like one of the English Sirdars or Pashas in Egypt. With him was his brother-in-law, lately come from Canada, a big and rather boisterous young gentleman-farmer, with a yellow beard, by name James Blount. With him also was the more insignificant figure of the priest from the neighbouring Roman Church; for the colonel's late wife had been a Catholic, and the children, as is common in such cases, had been trained to follow her. Everything seemed undistinguished about the priest, even down to his name, which was Brown; yet the colonel had always found something companionable about him, and frequently asked him to such family gatherings.

In the large entrance hall of the house there was ample room even for Sir Leopold and the removal of his wraps. Porch and vestibule, indeed, were unduly large in proportion to the house, and formed, as it were, a big room with the front door at one end, and the bottom of the staircase at the other. In front of the large hall fire, over which hung the colonel's sword, the process was completed and the company, including the saturnine Crook, presented to Sir Leopold Fischer. That venerable financier, however, still seemed to be struggling with portions of his well-lined attire, and at length produced from a very interior tail-coat pocket a black oval case which he radiantly explained to be his Christmas present for his god-daughter. With an unaffected vainglory that had something disarming about it he held out the case before them all; it flew open at a touch and half-blinded them. It was just as if a crystal fountain had spurted in their eyes. In a nest of orange velvet lay like three eggs, three white and vivid diamonds that seemed to set the very air on fire all round them. Fischer stood beaming benevolently and drinking deep of the astonishment and ecstasy of the girl, the grim admiration and gruff thanks of the colonel, the wonder of the whole group.

'I'll put 'em back now, my dear,' said Fischer, returning the case to the tails of his coat. 'I had to be careful of 'em coming down. They're the three great African diamonds called "The Flying Stars", because they've been stolen so often. All the big criminals are on the track; but even the rough men about in the streets and hotels could hardly have kept their hands off them. I might have lost them on the road here. It was quite possible.'

'Quite natural, I should say,' growled the man in the red tie. 'I shouldn't blame 'em if they had taken 'em. When they ask for bread, and you don't even give them a stone, I think they might take the stone for themselves.'

'I won't have you talking like that,' cried the girl, who was in a curious glow. 'You've only talked like that since you became a horrid what's-his-name. You know what I mean. What do you call a man who wants to embrace the chimney-sweep?'

'A saint,' said Father Brown.

'I think,' said Sir Leopold, with a supercilious smile, 'that Ruby means a Socialist.'

'A radical does not mean a man who lives on radishes,' remarked Crook, with some impatience; 'and a Conservative does not mean a man who preserves jam. Neither, I assure you, does a Socialist mean a man who desires a social evening with the chimney-sweep. A Socialist means a man who wants all the chimneys swept and all the chimney-sweeps paid for it.'

'But who won't allow you,' put in the priest in a low voice, 'to own your own soot.'

Crook looked at him with an eye of interest and even respect. 'Does one want to own soot?' he asked.

'One might,' answered Brown, with speculation in his eye. 'I've heard that gardeners use it. And I once made six children happy at Christmas when the conjuror didn't come, entirely with soot – applied externally.'

'Oh, splendid,' cried Ruby. 'Oh, I wish you'd do it to this company.'

The boisterous Canadian, Mr Blount, was lifting his loud voice in applause, and the astonished financier his (in some considerable deprecation), when a knock sounded at the double front doors. The priest opened them, and they showed again the front garden of evergreens, monkey tree and all, now gathering gloom against a gorgeous violet sunset. The scene thus framed was so coloured and quaint, like a back scene in a play, that they forgot a moment the insignificant figure standing in the door.

He was dusty-looking and in a frayed coat, evidently a common messenger. 'Any of you gentlemen Mr Blount?' he asked, and held forward a letter doubtfully. Mr Blount started, and stopped in his shout of assent. Ripping up the envelope with evident astonishment he read it; his face clouded a little, and then cleared, and he turned to his brother-in-law and host.

'I'm sick at being such a nuisance, colonel,' he said, with the cheery colonial conventions; 'but would it upset you if an old acquaintance called on me here tonight on business? In point of fact it's Florian, that famous French acrobat and comic actor; I knew him years ago out West (he was a French-Canadian by birth), and he seems to have business for me, though I hardly guess what.'

'Of course, of course,' replied the colonel carelessly. 'My dear chap, any friend of yours. No doubt he will prove an acquisition.'

'He'll black his face, if that's what you mean,' cried Blount, laughing. 'I don't doubt he'd black everyone else's eyes. I don't care; I'm not refined. I like the jolly old pantomime where a man sits on his top hat.'

'Not on mine, please,' said Sir Leopold Fischer, with dignity.

'Well, well,' observed Crook, airily, 'don't let's quarrel. There are lower jokes than sitting on a top hat.'

Dislike of the red-tied youth, born of his predatory

opinions and evident intimacy with the pretty godchild, led Fischer to say, in his most sarcastic, magisterial manner: 'No doubt you have found something much lower than sitting on a top hat. What is it, pray?'

'Letting a top hat sit on you, for instance,' said the Socialist.

'Now, now, now,' cried the Canadian farmer with his barbarian benevolence, 'don't let's spoil a jolly evening. What I say is, let's do something for the company tonight. Not blacking faces or sitting on hats, if you don't like those – but something of the sort. Why couldn't we have a proper old English pantomime – clown, columbine, and so on. I saw one when I left England at twelve years old, and it's blazed in my brain like a bonfire ever since. I came back to the old country only last year, and I find the thing's extinct. Nothing but a lot of snivelling fairy plays. I want a hot poker and a policeman made into sausages, and they give me princesses moralising by moonlight, Blue Birds, or something. Blue Beard's more in my line, and him I like best when he turned into the pantaloon.'

'I'm all for making a policeman into sausages,' said John Crook. 'It's a better definition of Socialism than some recently given. But surely the get-up would be too big a business.'

'Not a scrap,' cried Blount, quite carried away. 'A harlequinade's the quickest thing we can do, for two reasons.

First, one can gag to any degree; and, second, all the objects are household things – tables and towel-horses and washing baskets, and things like that.'

'That's true,' admitted Crook, nodding eagerly and walking about. 'But I'm afraid I can't have my policeman's uniform. Haven't killed a policeman lately.'

Blount frowned thoughtfully a space, and then smote his thigh. 'Yes, we can!' he cried. 'I've got Florian's address here, and he knows every costumier in London. I'll phone him to bring a police dress when he comes.' And he went bounding away to the telephone.

'Oh, it's glorious, godfather,' cried Ruby, almost dancing. 'I'll be columbine and you shall be pantaloon.'

The millionaire held himself stiff with a sort of heathen solemnity. 'I think, my dear,' he said, 'you must get someone else for pantaloon.'

'I will be pantaloon, if you like,' said Colonel Adams, taking his cigar out of his mouth, and speaking for the first and last time.

'You ought to have a statue,' cried the Canadian, as he came back, radiant, from the telephone. 'There, we are all fitted. Mr Crook shall be clown; he's a journalist and knows all the oldest jokes. I can be harlequin, that only wants long legs and jumping about. My friend Florian 'phones he's bringing the police costume; he's changing on the way. We can act it in this very hall, the audience sitting on those broad stairs opposite, one row above another. These front doors can be the back scene, either open or shut. Shut, you see an English interior. Open, a moonlit garden. It all goes by magic.' And snatching a chance piece of billiard chalk from his pocket, he ran it across the hall floor, halfway between the front door and the staircase, to mark the line of the footlights.

How even such a banquet of bosh was got ready in the time remained a riddle. But they went at it with that mixture of recklessness and industry that lives when youth is in a house; and youth was in that house that night, though not all may have isolated the two faces and hearts from which it flamed. As always happens, the invention grew wilder and wilder through the very tameness of the bourgeois conventions from which it had to create. The columbine looked charming in an outstanding skirt that strangely resembled the large lamp-shade in the drawing-room. The clown and pantaloon made themselves white with flour from the cook, and red with rouge from some other domestic, who remained (like all true Christian benefactors) anonymous. The harlequin, already clad in silver paper out of cigar boxes, was, with difficulty, prevented from smashing the old Victorian lustre chandeliers, that he might cover himself with resplendent crystals. In fact, he would certainly have done so, had not Ruby unearthed some old pantomime paste jewels she had worn at a fancy dress party as the Queen of Diamonds. Indeed, her uncle, James Blount, was getting almost out of hand in his excitement; he was like a schoolboy. He put a paper donkey's head unexpectedly on Father Brown, who bore it patiently, and even found some private manner of moving his ears. He even essayed to put the paper donkey's tail to the coat-tails of Sir Leopold Fischer. This, however, was frowned down. 'Uncle is too absurd,' cried Ruby to Crook, round whose shoulders she had seriously placed a string of sausages. 'Why is he so wild?'

'He is harlequin to your columbine,' said Crook. 'I am only the clown who makes the old jokes.'

'I wish you were the harlequin,' she said, and left the string of sausages swinging.

Father Brown, though he knew every detail done behind the scenes, and had even evoked applause by his transformation of a pillow into a pantomime baby, went round to the front and sat among the audience with all the solemn expectation of a child at his first matinee. The spectators were few, relations, one or two local friends, and the servants; Sir Leopold sat in the front seat, his full and still fur-collared figure largely obscuring the view of the little cleric behind him; but it has never been settled by artistic authorities whether the cleric lost much. The pantomime was utterly chaotic, yet not contemptible; there ran through it a rage of improvisation which came chiefly from Crook the clown. Commonly he was a clever man, and he was inspired tonight with a wild omniscience, a folly wiser than the world, that which comes to a young man who has seen for an instant a particular expression on a particular face. He was supposed to be the clown, but he was really almost everything else, the author (so far as there was an author), the prompter, the scene-painter, the scene-shifter, and, above all, the orchestra. At abrupt intervals in the outrageous performance he would hurl himself in full costume at the piano and bang out some popular music equally absurd and appropriate.

The climax of this, as of all else, was the moment when the two front doors at the back of the scene flew open, showing the lovely moonlit garden, but showing more prominently the famous professional guest; the great Florian, dressed up as a policeman. The clown at the piano played the constabulary chorus in the 'Pirates of Penzance', but it was drowned in the deafening applause, for every gesture of the great comic actor was an admirable though restrained version of the carriage and manner of the police. The harlequin leapt upon him and hit him over the helmet; the pianist playing 'Where did you get that hat?' he faced about in admirably simulated astonishment, and then the leaping harlequin hit him again (the pianist suggesting a few bars of 'Then we had another one'). Then the harlequin rushed right into the arms of the policeman and fell on top of him, amid a roar of applause. Then it was that the strange actor gave that celebrated imitation of a dead man, of which the fame still lingers round Putney. It was almost impossible to believe that a living person could appear so limp.

The athletic harlequin swung him about like a sack or twisted or tossed him like an Indian club; all the time to the most maddeningly ludicrous tunes from the piano. When the harlequin heaved the comic constable heavily off the floor the clown played 'I arise from dreams of thee'. When he shuffled him across his back, 'With my bundle on my shoulder', and when the harlequin finally let fall the policeman with a most convincing thud, the lunatic at the instrument struck into a jingling measure with some words which are still believed to have been, 'I sent a letter to my love and on the way I dropped it'.

At about this limit of mental anarchy Father Brown's view was obscured altogether; for the City magnate in front of him rose to his full height and thrust his hands savagely into all his pockets. Then he sat down nervously, still fumbling, and then stood up again. For an instant it seemed seriously likely that he would stride across the footlights; then he turned a glare at the clown playing the piano; and then he burst in silence out of the room.

The priest had only watched for a few more minutes the absurd but not inelegant dance of the amateur harlequin over his splendidly unconscious foe. With real though rude art, the harlequin danced slowly backwards out of the door into the garden, which was full of moonlight and stillness. The vamped dress of silver paper and paste, which had been too glaring in the footlights, looked more and more magical and silvery as it danced away under a brilliant moon. The audience was closing in with a cataract of applause, when Brown felt his arm abruptly touched, and he was asked in a whisper to come into the colonel's study.

He followed his summoner with increasing doubt, which was not dispelled by a solemn comicality in the scene of the study. There sat Colonel Adams, still unaffectedly dressed as a pantaloon, with the knobbed whalebone nodding above his brow, but with his poor old eyes sad enough to have sobered a Saturnalia. Sir Leopold Fischer was leaning against the mantelpiece and heaving with all the importance of panic.

'This is a very painful matter, Father Brown,' said Adams. 'The truth is, those diamonds we all saw this afternoon seem to have vanished from my friend's tail-coat pocket. And as you—'

'As I,' supplemented Father Brown, with a broad grin, 'was sitting just behind him—'

'Nothing of the sort shall be suggested,' said Colonel Adams, with a firm look at Fischer, which rather implied that some such thing had been suggested. 'I only ask you to give me the assistance that any gentleman might give.'

'Which is turning out his pockets,' said Father Brown, and proceeded to do so, displaying seven and sixpence, a return ticket, a small silver crucifix, a small breviary and a stick of chocolate.

The colonel looked at him long, and then said, 'Do you know, I should like to see the inside of your head more than the inside of your pockets. My daughter is one of your people, I know; well, she has lately—' and he stopped.

'She has lately,' cried out old Fischer, 'opened her father's house to a cut-throat Socialist, who says openly he would steal anything from a richer man. This is the end of it. Here is the richer man – and none the richer.'

'If you want the inside of my head you can have it,' said Brown rather wearily. 'What it's worth you can say afterwards. But the first thing I find in that disused pocket is this: that men who mean to steal diamonds don't talk Socialism. They are more likely,' he added demurely, 'to denounce it.'

Both the others shifted sharply and the priest went on:

'You see, we know these people, more or less. That Socialist would no more steal a diamond than a pyramid. We ought to look at once to the one man we don't know. The fellow acting the policeman – Florian. Where is he exactly at this minute, I wonder.'

The pantaloon sprang erect and strode out of the room. An interlude ensued, during which the millionaire stared at the priest, and the priest at his breviary; then the pantaloon returned and said, with staccato gravity, 'The policeman is still lying on the stage. The curtain has gone up and down six times; he is still lying there.'

Father Brown dropped his book and stood staring with a look of blank mental ruin. Very slowly a light began to creep in his grey eyes, and then he made the scarcely obvious answer.

'Please forgive me, colonel, but when did your wife die?'

'Wife!' replied the staring soldier, 'she died this year two months. Her brother James arrived just a week too late to see her.'

The little priest bounded like a rabbit shot. 'Come on!' he cried in quite unusual excitement. 'Come on! We've got to go and look at that policeman!'

They rushed on to the now curtained stage, breaking rudely past the columbine and clown (who seemed whispering quite contentedly), and Father Brown bent over the prostrate comic policeman.

'Chloroform,' he said as he rose; 'I only guessed it just now.'

There was a startled stillness, and then the colonel said slowly, 'Please say seriously what all this means.'

Father Brown suddenly shouted with laughter, then stopped, and only struggled with it for instants during the rest of his speech. 'Gentlemen,' he gasped, 'there's not much time to talk. I must run after the criminal. But this great French actor who played the policeman – this clever corpse the harlequin waltzed with and dandled and threw about – he was—' His voice again failed him, and he turned his back to run.

'He was?' called Fischer inquiringly.

'A real policeman,' said Father Brown, and ran away into the dark.

There were hollows and bowers at the extreme end of that leafy garden, in which the laurels and other immortal shrubs showed against sapphire sky and silver moon, even in that midwinter, warm colours as of the south. The green gaiety of the waving laurels, the rich purple indigo of the night, the moon like a monstrous crystal, make an almost irresponsible romantic picture; and among the top branches of the garden trees a strange figure is climbing, who looks not so much romantic as impossible. He sparkles from head to heel, as if clad in ten million moons; the real moon catches him at every movement and sets a new inch of him on fire. But he swings, flashing and successful, from the short tree in this garden to the tall, rambling tree in the other, and only stops there because a shade has slid under the smaller tree and has unmistakably called up to him.

'Well, Flambeau,' says the voice, 'you really look like a Flying Star; but that always means a Falling Star at last.'

The silver, sparkling figure above seems to lean forward in the laurels and, confident of escape, listens to the little figure below.

'You never did anything better, Flambeau. It was clever to come from Canada (with a Paris ticket, I suppose) just a week after Mrs Adams died, when no one was in a mood to ask questions. It was cleverer to have marked down the Flying Stars and the very day of Fischer's coming. But there's no cleverness, but mere genius, in what followed. Stealing the stones, I suppose, was nothing to you. You could have done it by sleight of hand in a hundred other ways besides that pretence of putting a paper donkey's tail to Fischer's coat. But in the rest you eclipsed yourself.'

The silvery figure among the green leaves seems to linger as if hypnotised, though his escape is easy behind him; he is staring at the man below.

'Oh, yes,' says the man below, 'I know all about it. I know you not only forced the pantomime, but put it to a double use. You were going to steal the stones quietly; news came by an accomplice that you were already suspected, and a capable police officer was coming to rout you up that very night. A common thief would have been thankful for the warning and fled; but you are a poet. You already had the clever notion of hiding the jewels in a blaze of false stage jewellery. Now, you saw that if the dress were a harlequin's the appearance of a policeman would be quite in keeping. The worthy officer started from Putney police station to find you, and walked into the queerest trap ever set in this world. When the front door opened he walked straight on to the stage of a Christmas pantomime, where he could be kicked, clubbed, stunned and drugged by the dancing harlequin, amid roars of laughter from all the most respectable people in Putney. Oh, you will never do anything better. And now, by the way, you might give me back those diamonds.'

The green branch on which the glittering figure swung, rustled as if in astonishment; but the voice went on:

'I want you to give them back, Flambeau, and I want you to give up this life. There is still youth and honour and humour in you; don't fancy they will last in that trade. Men may keep a sort of level of good, but no man has ever been able to keep on one level of evil. That road goes down and down. The kind man drinks and turns cruel; the frank man kills and lies about it. Many a man I've known started like you to be an honest outlaw, a merry robber of the rich, and ended stamped into slime. Maurice Blum started out as an anarchist of principle, a father of the poor; he ended a greasy spy and tale-bearer that both sides used and despised. Harry Burke started his free money movement sincerely enough; now he's sponging on a half-starved sister for endless brandies and sodas. Lord Amber went into wild society in a sort of chivalry; now he's paying blackmail to the lowest vultures in London. Captain Barillon was the great gentleman-apache before your time; he died in a madhouse, screaming with fear of the "narks" and receivers that had betrayed him and hunted him down. I know the woods look very free behind you, Flambeau; I know that in a flash you could melt into them like a monkey. But some day you will be an old grey monkey, Flambeau. You will sit up in your free forest cold at heart and close to death, and the tree-tops will be very bare.'

Everything continued still, as if the small man below held the other in the tree in some long invisible leash; and he went on:

'Your downward steps have begun. You used to boast of doing nothing mean, but you are doing something mean tonight. You are leaving suspicion on an honest boy with a good deal against him already; you are separating him from the woman he loves and who loves him. But you will do meaner things than that before you die.'

Three flashing diamonds fell from the tree to the turf. The small man stooped to pick them up, and when he looked up again the green cage of the tree was emptied of its silver bird.

The restoration of the gems (accidentally picked up

by Father Brown, of all people) ended the evening in uproarious triumph; and Sir Leopold, in his height of good humour, even told the priest that though he himself had broader views, he could respect those whose creed required them to be cloistered and ignorant of this world.

A Problem In White

Nicholas Blake

'Seasonable weather for the time of year,' remarked the
Expansive Man in a voice succulent as the breast of a roast
goose.

The Deep Chap, sitting next to him in the railway compartment, glanced out at the snow swarming and swirling
past the window-pane. He replied:

'You really like it? Oh well, it's an ill blizzard that blows
nobody no good. Depends what you mean by seasonable,
though. Statistics for the last fifty years would show—'

'Name of Joad, sir?' asked the Expansive Man, treating
the compartment to a wholesale wink.

'No, Stansfield, Henry Stansfield.' The Deep Chap,
a ruddy-faced man who sat with hands firmly planted
on the knees of his brown tweed suit, might have been

a prosperous farmer but for the long, steady meditative scrutiny which he now bent upon each of his fellow travellers in turn.

What he saw was not particularly rewarding. On the opposite seat, from left to right, were a Forward Piece, who had taken the Expansive Man's wink wholly to herself and contrived to wriggle her tight skirt farther up from her knee; a desiccated, sandy, lawyerish little man who fumed and fussed like an angry kettle, consulting every five minutes his gold watch, then shaking out his *Times* with the crackle of a legal parchment, and a Flash Card, dressed up to the nines of spivdom, with the bold yet uneasy stare of the young delinquent.

'Mine's Percy Dukes,' said the Expansive Man. 'P.D. to my friends, General Dealer. At your service. Well, we'll be across the border in an hour and a half, and then hey for the bluebells of bonny Scotland!'

'Bluebells in January? You're hopeful,' remarked the Forward Piece.

'Are you Scots, master?' asked the Comfortable Body sitting on Stansfield's left.

'English outside' – Percy Dukes patted the front of his grey suit, slid a flask from its hip pocket, and took a swig – 'and Scotch within.' His loud laugh, or the blizzard, shook the railway carriage. The Forward Piece giggled. The Flash Card covertly sneered.

'You'll need that if we run into a drift and get stuck for the night,' said Henry Stansfield.

'Name of Jonah, sir?' The compartment reverberated again.

'I do not apprehend such an eventuality,' said the Fusspot. 'The station-master at Lancaster assured me that the train would get through. We are scandalously late already, though.' Once again the gold watch was consulted.

'It's a curious thing,' remarked the Deep Chap meditatively, 'the way we imagine we can make Time amble withal or gallop withal, just by keeping an eye on the hands of a watch. You travel frequently by this train, Mr—?'

'Kilmington. Arthur J. Kilmington. No, I've only used it once before.' The Fusspot spoke in a dry Edinburgh accent.

'Ah yes, that would have been on the 17th of last month. I remember seeing you on it.'

'No, sir, you are mistaken. It was the 20th.' Mr Kilmington's thin mouth snapped tight again, like a rubber band round a sheaf of legal documents.

'The 20th? Indeed? That was the day of the train robbery. A big haul they got, it seems. Off this very train. It was carrying some of the extra Christmas mail. Bags just disappeared, somewhere between Lancaster and Carlisle.'

'Och, deary me,' sighed the Comfortable Body. 'I don't know what we're coming to, really, nowadays.'

'We're coming to the scene of the crime, ma'am,' said the expansive Mr Dukes. The train, almost dead-beat, was panting up the last pitch towards Shap Summit.

'I didn't see anything in the papers about where the robbery took place,' Henry Stansfield murmured. Dukes fastened a somewhat bleary eye upon him.

'You read all the newspapers?'

'Yes.'

The atmosphere in the compartment had grown suddenly tense. Only the Flash Card, idly examining his fingernails, seemed unaffected by it.

'Which paper did you see it in?' pursued Stansfield.

'I didn't.' Dukes tapped Stansfield on the knee. 'But I can use my loaf. Stands to reason. You want to tip a mail-bag out of a train – get me? Train must be moving slowly, or the bag'll burst when it hits the ground. Only one place between Lancaster and Carlisle where you'd *know* the train would be crawling. Shap Bank. And it goes slowest on the last bit of the bank, just about where we are now. Follow?'

Henry Stansfield nodded.

'OK. But you'd be barmy to tip it off just anywhere on this God-forsaken moorland,' went on Mr Dukes. 'Now, if you'd travelled this line as much as I have, you'd have noticed it goes over a bridge about a mile short of the summit. Under the bridge runs a road: a nice, lonely road, see? The only road hereabouts that touches the railway. You tip out the bag there. Your chums collect it, run down the embankment, dump it in the car they've got waiting by the bridge, and Bob's your uncle!'

'You oughta been a detective, mister,' exclaimed the Forward Piece languishingly.

Mr Dukes inserted his thumbs in his armpits, looking gratified. 'Maybe I am,' he said with a wheezy laugh. 'And maybe I'm just little old P.D., who knows how to use his loaf.'

'Och, well now, the things people will do!' said the Comfortable Body. 'There's a terrible lot of dishonesty today.'

The Flash Card glanced up contemptuously from his fingernails. Mr Kilmington was heard to mutter that the system of surveillance on railways was disgraceful, and the Guard of the train should have been severely censured.

'The Guard can't be everywhere,' said Stansfield. 'Presumably he has to patrol the train from time to time, and—'

'Let him do so, then, and not lock himself up in his van and go to sleep,' interrupted Mr Kilmington, somewhat unreasonably.

'Are you speaking from personal experience, sir?' asked Stansfield.

The Flash Card lifted up his voice and said, in a Charing-Cross-Road American accent, 'Hey, fellas! If the gang was gonna tip out the mail-bags by the bridge, like this guy says – what I mean is, how could they rely on the Guard being out of his van just at that point?' He hitched up the trousers of his loud check suit.

'You've got something there,' said Percy Dukes. 'What I reckon is, there must have been two accomplices on the train – one to get the Guard out of his van on some pretext, and the other to chuck off the bags.' He turned to Mr Kilmington. 'You were saying something about the Guard locking himself up in his van. Now if I was of a suspicious turn of mind, if I was little old Sherlock H. in person' – he bestowed another prodigious wink upon Kilmington's fellow travellers – 'I'd begin to wonder about you, sir. You were travelling on this train when the robbery took place. You went to the Guard's van. You *say* you found him asleep. You didn't by any chance call the Guard out, so as to——?'

'Your suggestion is outrageous! I advise you to be very careful, sir, very careful indeed,' enunciated Mr Kilmington, his precise voice crackling with indignation, 'or you may find you have said something actionable. I would have you know that, when I——'

But what he would have them know was to remain undivulged. The train, which for some little time had been running cautiously down from Shap Summit, suddenly began to chatter and shudder, like a fever patient in high delirium, as the vacuum brakes were applied; then, with the dull impact of a fist driving into a feather pillow, the engine buried itself in a drift which had gathered just beyond the bend of a deep cutting. The time was five minutes past seven.

'What's this in aid of?' asked the Forward Piece, rather shrilly, as a hysterical outburst of huffing and puffing came from the engine.

'Run into a drift, I reckon.'

'He's trying to back us out. No good. The wheels are slipping every time. What a lark!' Percy Dukes had his head out of the window on the lee side of the train. 'Coom to Coomberland for your winter sports!'

'Guard! Guard, I say!' called Mr Kilmington. But the blue-clad figure, after one glance into the compartment, hurried on his way up the corridor. 'Really! I *shall* report that man.'

Henry Stansfield, going out into the corridor, opened a window. Though the coach was theoretically sheltered by the cutting on this windward side, the blizzard stunned his face like a knuckleduster of ice. He joined the herd of passengers who had climbed down and were stumbling towards the engine. As they reached it, the Guard emerged from its cab: no cause for alarm, he said; if they couldn't get through, there'd be a relief engine sent down to take the train back to Tebay; he was just off to set fog-signals on the line behind them.

The driver renewed his attempts to back the train out. But, what with its weight, the up-gradient in its rear, the icy rails, and the clinging grip of the drift on the engine, he could not budge her.

'We'll have to dig out the bogeys, mate,' he said to the fireman. 'Fetch them shovels from the forward van. It'll keep the perishers from freezing, any road.' He jerked his finger at the knot of passengers who, lit up by the glare of the furnace, were capering and beating their arms like savages amid the swirling snow-wreaths.

Percy Dukes, who had now joined them, quickly established himself as the life and soul of the party, referring to the grimy-faced fireman as 'Snowball', adjuring his companions to 'Dig for Victory', affecting to spy the approach of a herd of St Bernards, each with a keg of brandy slung round its neck. But, after ten minutes of hard digging, when the leading wheels of the bogey were cleared, it could be seen that they had been derailed by their impact with the drift.

'That's torn it, Charlie. You'll have to walk back to the box and get 'em to telephone through for help,' said the driver.

'*If* the wires aren't down already,' replied the fireman lugubriously. 'It's above a mile to that box, and uphill. Who d'you think I am? Captain Scott?'

'You'll have the wind behind you, mate, any road. So long.' A buzz of dismay had risen from the passengers at this. One or two, who began to get querulous, were silenced by the driver's offering to take them anywhere they liked if they would just lift his engine back on to the metals first. When the rest had dispersed to their carriages, Henry Stansfield asked the driver's permission to go up into the cab for a few minutes and dry his coat.

'You're welcome.' The driver snorted: 'Would you believe it? "Must get to Glasgow tonight." Damn ridiculous! Now Bert – that's my Guard – it's different for him: he's entitled to fret a bit. Missus been very poorly. Thought she was going to peg out before Christmas; but he got the best surgeon in Glasgow to operate on her, and she's mending now, he says. He reckons to look in every night at the nursing home, when he goes off work.'

Stansfield chatted with the man for five minutes. Then the Guard returned, blowing upon his hands – a smallish, leathery-faced chap, with an anxious look in his eye.

'We'll not get through tonight, Bert. Charlie told you?'

'Aye. I doubt some of the passengers are going to create a rumpus,' said the Guard dolefully.

Henry Stansfield went back to his compartment. It was

stuffy, but with a sinister hint of chilliness, too: he wondered how long the steam heating would last: depended upon the amount of water in the engine boiler, he supposed. Amongst the wide variety of fates he had imagined for himself, freezing to death in an English train was not included.

Arthur J. Kilmington fidgeted more than ever. When the Guard came along the corridor, he asked him where the nearest village was, saying he must get a telephone call through to Edinburgh – most urgent appointment – must let his client know, if he was going to miss it. The Guard said there was a village two miles to the north-east; you could see the lights from the top of the cutting; but he warned Mr Kilmington against trying to get there in the teeth of this blizzard – better wait for the relief engine, which should reach them before 9 p.m.

Silence fell upon the compartment for a while; the incredulous silence of civilised people who find themselves in the predicament of castaways. Then the expansive Mr Dukes proposed that, since they were to be stuck here for an hour or two, they should get acquainted. The Comfortable Body now introduced herself as Mrs Grant, the Forward Piece as Inez Blake; the Flash Card, with the over-negligent air of one handing a dud half-crown over a counter, gave his name as Macdonald – I. Macdonald.

'A fine old Scots name,' said Mrs Grant.

'I for Ian,' said Mr Dukes. 'Or would it be Izzy?'

'Irving, if you want to know,' replied the young man. 'Any objection? You like to make something of it?'

'Keep your hair on, young shaver.'

'So I'm a Yid, am I? That's your idea, uh?'

'If you get steamed up any more,' said Mr Dukes, 'it'll ruin that permanent wave of yours.'

'It only remains for one of you to suggest a nice friendly game of cards, now we've had the preliminary patter,' said Henry Stansfield.

This reference to the technique of card-sharpers who work the trains silenced even Percy Dukes for a moment. However, he soon recovered.

'I see you weren't born yesterday, mister. We must've sounded a bit like that. You can always tell 'em a mile off, can't you? No offence meant to this young gent. Just P.D.'s little bit of fun.'

'I wish somebody would tell me what this is all about,' asked Inez Blake, pouting provocatively at Mr Dukes, who at once obliged.

'They must be awfu' clever,' remarked Mrs Grant, in her sing-song Lowland accent, when he had finished.

'No criminals are clever, ma'am,' said Stansfield quietly. His ruminative eye passed, without haste, from Macdonald to Dukes. 'Neither the small fry nor the big operators. They're pretty well subhuman, the whole lot of 'em. A dash of cunning, a thick streak of cowardice, and the rest is made up of stupidity and boastfulness. They're too stupid for anything but crime, and so riddled with inferiority that they always give themselves away, sooner or later, by boasting about their crimes. They like to think of themselves as the wide boys, but they're as narrow as starved eels – why, they haven't even the wits to alter their professional methods: that's how the police pick 'em up.'

'I entirely agree, sir,' Mr Kilmington snapped. 'In my profession I see a good deal of the criminal classes. And I flatter myself none of them has ever got the better of me. They're transparent, sir, transparent.'

'No doubt you gentlemen are right,' said Percy Dukes comfortably. 'But the police haven't picked up the chaps who did this train robbery yet.'

'They will. And the Countess of Axminster's emerald bracelet. Bet the gang didn't reckon to find that in the mail-bag. Worth all of £25,000.'

Percy Duke's mouth fell open. The Flash Card whistled. Overcome, either by the stuffiness of the carriage or the thought of £25,000-worth of emeralds, Inez Blake gave a little moan and fainted all over Mr Kilmington's lap.

'Really! Upon my soul! My dear young lady!' exclaimed that worthy. There was a flutter of solicitude, shared by all except the cold-eyed young Macdonald who, after stooping over her a moment, his back to the others, said, 'Here you – stop pawing the young lady and let her stretch out on the seat. Yes, I'm talking to you, Kilmington.'

'How dare you! This is an outrage!' The little man stood up so abruptly that the girl was almost rolled on to the floor. 'I was merely trying to—'

'I know your sort. Nasty old men. Now, keep your hands off her! I'm telling you.'

In the shocked silence that ensued, Kilmington gobbled speechlessly at Macdonald for a moment; then, seeing razors in the youth's cold-steel eye, snatched his black hat and brief-case from the rack and bolted out of the compartment. Henry Stansfield made as if to stop him, then changed his mind. Mrs Grant followed the little man out, returning presently, her handkerchief soaked in water, to dab Miss Blake's forehead. The time was just on 8.30.

When things were restored to normal, Mr Dukes turned to Stansfield. 'You were saying this necklace of – who was it? – the Countess of Axminster, it's worth £25,000? Fancy sending a thing of that value through the post! Are you sure of it?'

'The value? Oh, yes.' Henry Stansfield spoke out of the corner of his mouth, in the manner of a stupid man imparting a confidence. 'Don't let this go any farther. But I've a friend who works in the Cosmopolitan – the Company where it's insured. That's another thing that didn't get into the papers. Silly woman. She wanted it for some big family do in Scotland at Christmas, forgot to bring it with her, and wrote home for it to be posted to her in a registered packet.'

'£25,000,' said Percy Dukes thoughtfully. 'Well, stone me down!'

'Yes. Some people don't know when they're lucky, do they?'

Dukes' fat face wobbled on his shoulders like a globe of lard. Young Macdonald polished his nails. Inez Blake read her magazine. After some while, Percy Dukes remarked that the blizzard was slackening; he'd take an airing and see if there was any sign of the relief engine yet. He left the compartment.

At the window, the snowflakes danced in their tens now, not their thousands. The time was 8.55. Shortly afterwards, Inez Blake went out; and ten minutes later, Mrs Grant remarked to Stansfield that it had stopped snowing altogether. Neither Inez nor Dukes had returned when, at 9.30, Henry Stansfield decided to ask what had happened about the relief. The Guard was not in his van, which adjoined Stansfield's coach, towards the rear of the train. So he turned back, walked up the corridor to the front coach, clambered out, and hailed the engine cab.

'She must have been held up,' said the Guard, leaning out. 'Charlie here got through from the box, and they promised her by nine o'clock. But it'll no' be long now, sir.'

'Have you seen anything of a Mr Kilmington – small, sandy chap – black hat and overcoat, blue suit – was in my compartment? I've walked right up the train and he doesn't seem to be on it.'

The Guard pondered a moment. 'Och aye, yon wee fellow? Him that asked me about telephoning from the village. Aye, he's awa' then.'

'He did set off to walk there, you mean?'

'Nae doot he did, if he's no' on the train. He spoke to me again – juist on nine, it'd be – and said he was awa' if the relief didna turn up in five minutes.'

'You've not seen him since?'

'No, sir. I've been talking to my mates here this half-hour, ever syne the wee fellow spoke to me.'

Henry Stansfield walked thoughtfully back down the permanent way. When he had passed out of the glare shed by the carriage lights on the snow, he switched on his electric torch. Just beyond the last coach, the eastern wall of the cutting sloped sharply down and merged into moorland level with the track. Although the snow had stopped altogether, an icy wind from the north-east still blew, raking and numbing his face. Twenty yards farther on, his torch lit up a track, already half filled in with snow, made by several pairs of feet, pointing away over the moor, towards the north-east. Several passengers, it seemed, had set off for the village, whose lights twinkled like frost in the far distance. Stansfield was about to follow this track when he heard footsteps scrunching the snow farther up the line. He switched off the torch; at once it was as if a sack had been thrown over his head, so close and blinding was the darkness. The steps came nearer. Stansfield switched on his torch, at the last minute, pin-pointing the squab figure of Percy Dukes. The man gave a muffled oath.

'What the devil! Here, what's the idea, keeping me waiting half an hour in that blasted—?'

'Have you seen Kilmington?'

'Oh, it's you. No, how the hell should I have seen him? Isn't he on the train? I've been walking up the line, to look for the relief. No sign yet. Damn parky, it is – I'm moving on.'

Presently Stansfield moved on, too, but along the track towards the village. The circle of his torchlight wavered and bounced on the deep snow. The wind, right in his teeth, was killing. No wonder, he thought, as after a few hundred yards he approached the end of the trail, those passengers turned back. Then he realised they had not all turned back. What he had supposed to be a hummock of snow bearing a crude resemblance to a recumbent human figure, he now saw to be a human figure covered with snow. He scraped some of the snow off it, turned it gently over on its back.

Arthur J. Kilmington would fuss no more in this world. His brief-case was buried beneath him: his black hat was lying where it had fallen, lightly covered with snow, near the head. There seemed, to Stansfield's cursory examination, no mark of violence on him. But the eyeballs started, the face was suffused with a pinkish-blue colour. So men look who have been strangled, thought Stansfield, or asphyxiated. Quickly he knelt down again, shining his torch in the dead face. A qualm of horror shook him. Mr Kilmington's nostrils were caked thick with snow, which had frozen solid in them, and snow had been rammed tight into his mouth also.

And here he would have stayed, reflected Stansfield, in this desolate spot, for days or weeks, perhaps, if the snow lay or deepened. And when the thaw at last came (as it did that year, in fact, only after two months), the snow would thaw out from his mouth and nostrils, too, and there would be no vestige of murder left – only the corpse of an impatient little lawyer who had tried to walk to the village in a blizzard and died for his pains. It might even be that no one would ask how such a precise, pernickety little chap had ventured the two-mile walk in thin shoes and without a torch to light his way through the pitchy blackness; for Stansfield, going through the man's pockets, had found the following articles – and nothing more: pocket-book, fountain pen, handkerchief, cigarette-case, gold lighter, two letters and some loose change.

Stansfield started to return for help. But, only twenty yards back, he noticed another trail of footprints, leading off the main track to the left. This trail seemed a fresher one – the snow lay less thickly in the indentations – and to have been made by one pair of feet only. He followed it up, walking beside it. Whoever made this track had walked in a slight right-handed curve back to the railway line, joining it about 150 yards south of where the main trail came out. At this point there was a platelayers' shack. Finding the door unlocked, Stansfield entered. There was nothing inside but a coke-brazier, stone cold, and a smell of cigar smoke …

Half an hour later, Stansfield returned to his compartment. In the meanwhile, he had helped the train crew to carry back the body of Kilmington, which was now locked in the Guard's van. He had also made an interesting discovery as to Kilmington's movements. It was to be presumed that, after the altercation with Macdonald, and the brief conversation already reported by the Guard, the lawyer must have gone to sit in another compartment. The last coach, to the rear of the Guard's van, was a first-class one, almost empty. But in one of its compartments, Stansfield found a passenger asleep. He woke him up, gave a description of Kilmington, and asked if he had seen him earlier.

The passenger grumpily informed Stansfield that a smallish man, in a dark overcoat, with the trousers of a blue suit showing beneath it, had come to the door and had a word with him. No, the passenger had not noticed his face particularly, because he'd been very drowsy himself, and besides, the chap had politely taken off his black Homburg hat to address him, and the hat screened as much of the head as was not cut off from his view by the top of the door. No, the chap had not come into his compartment: he had just stood outside, inquired the time (the passenger had looked at his watch and told him it was 8.50); then the chap had said that, if the relief didn't turn up by nine, he intended to walk to the nearest village.

Stansfield had then walked along to the engine cab. The Guard, whom he found there, told him that he'd gone up the track about 8.45 to meet the fireman on his way back from the signal-box. He had gone as far as the place where he had put down his fog-signals earlier; here, just before nine, he and the fireman met, as the latter corroborated. Returning to the train, the Guard had climbed into the last coach, noticed Kilmington sitting alone in a first-class compartment (it was then that the lawyer announced to the Guard his intention of walking if the relief engine had not arrived within five minutes). The Guard then got out of the train again, and proceeded down the track to talk to his mates in the engine cab.

This evidence would seem to point incontrovertibly at Kilmington's having been murdered shortly after 9 p.m., Stansfield reflected as he went back to his own compartment. His other fellow passengers were all present and correct now.

'Well, did you find him?' asked Percy Dukes.

'Kilmington? Oh yes, I found him. In the snow over there. He was dead.'

Inez Blake gave a little, affected scream. The permanent sneer was wiped, as if by magic, off young Macdonald's face, which turned a sickly white. Mr Dukes sucked in his fat lips.

'The puir wee man,' said Mrs Grant. 'He tried to walk it then? Died of exposure, was it?'

'No,' announced Stansfield flatly, 'he was murdered.'

This time, Inez Blake screamed in earnest; and, like an echo, a hooting shriek came from far up the line: the relief engine was approaching at last.

'The police will be awaiting us back at Tebay, so we'd better all have our stories ready.' Stansfield turned to Percy Dukes. 'You, for instance, sir. Where were you between 8.55, when you left the carriage, and 9.35 when I met you returning? Are you sure you didn't see Kilmington?'

Dukes, expansive no longer, his piggy eyes sunk deep

in the fat of his face, asked Stansfield who the hell he thought he was.

'I am an inquiry agent, employed by the Cosmopolitan Insurance Company. Before that, I was a Detective Inspector in the C.I.D. Here is my card.'

Dukes barely glanced at it. 'That's all right, old man. Only wanted to make sure. Can't trust anyone nowadays.' His voice had taken on the ingratiating, oleaginous heartiness of the small businessman trying to clinch a deal with a bigger one. 'Just went for a stroll, y'know – stretch the old legs. Didn't see a soul.'

'Who were you expecting to see? Didn't you wait for someone in the platelayers' shack along there, and smoke a cigar while you were waiting? Who did you mistake me for when you said "What's the idea, keeping me waiting half an hour"?'

'Here, draw it mild, old man.' Percy Dukes sounded injured. 'I certainly looked in at the hut: smoked a cigar for a bit. Then I toddled back to the train, and met up with your good self on the way. I didn't make no appointment to meet—'

'Oo! Well I *must* say,' interrupted Miss Blake virtuously. She could hardly wait to tell Stansfield that, on leaving the compartment shortly after Dukes, she'd overheard voices on the track below the lavatory window. 'I recognised this gentleman's voice,' she went on, tossing her head at Dukes. 'He said something like, "You're going to help us again, chum, so you'd better get used to the idea. You're in it up to the neck – can't back out now." And another voice, sort of mumbling, might have been Mr Kilmington's – I dunno – sounded Scotch anyway – said, "All right. Meet you in five minutes: platelayers' hut a few hundred yards up the line. Talk it over."'

'And what did you do then, young lady?' asked Stansfield. 'You didn't return to the compartment, I remember.'

'I happened to meet a gentleman friend, farther up the train, and sat with him for a bit.'

'Is that so?' remarked Macdonald menacingly. 'Why, you four-flushing little—!'

'Shut up!' commanded Stansfield.

'Honest I did,' the girl said, ignoring Macdonald. 'I'll introduce you to him, if you like. He'll tell you I was with him for, oh, half an hour or more.'

'And what about Mr Macdonald?'

'I'm not talking,' said the youth sullenly.

'Mr Macdonald isn't talking. Mrs Grant?'

'I've been in this compartment ever since, sir.'

'Ever since—?'

'Since I went out to damp my hankie for this young lady, when she'd fainted. Mr Kilmington was just before me, you'll mind. I saw him go through into the Guard's van.'

'Did you hear him say anything about walking to the village?'

'No, sir. He just hurried into the van, and then there was some havers about it's no' being lockit this time, and how he was going to report the Guard for it – I didna listen any more, wishing to get back to the young lady. I doubt the wee man would be for reporting everyone.'

'I see. And you've been sitting here with Mr Macdonald all the time?'

'Yes, sir. Except for ten minutes or so he was out of the compartment, just after you'd left.'

'What did you go out for?' Stansfield asked the young man.

'Just taking the air, brother, just taking the air.'

'You weren't taking Mr Kilmington's gold watch, as well as the air, by any chance?' Stansfield's keen eyes were fastened like a hook into Macdonald's, whose insolent expression visibly crumbled beneath them.

'I don't know what you mean,' he tried to bluster. 'You can't do this to me.'

'I mean that a man has been murdered: and, when the police search you, they will find his gold watch in your possession. Won't look too healthy for you, my young friend.'

'Naow! Give us a chance! It was only a joke, see?' The wretched Macdonald was whining now in his native cockney. 'He got me riled – the stuck-up way he said nobody'd ever got the better of him. So I thought I'd just show him – I'd have given it back, straight I would, only I couldn't find him afterwards. It was just a joke, I tell you. Anyway, it was Inez who lifted the ticker.'

'You dirty little rotter!' screeched the girl.

'Shut up, both of you! You can explain your joke to the police. Let's hope they don't die laughing.'

At this moment the train gave a lurch, and started back up the gradient. It halted at the signal-box, for Stansfield to telephone to Tebay, then clattered south again.

On Tebay platform, Stansfield was met by an Inspector and a Sergeant of the County Constabulary, with the Police Surgeon. No passengers were permitted to alight till he had had a few words with them. Then the four men boarded the train. After a brief pause in the Guard's van, where the Police Surgeon drew aside the Guard's black off-duty overcoat that had been laid over the body, and began his preliminary examination, they marched along to Stansfield's compartment. The Guard who, at his request, had locked this as the train was drawing up at the platform and was keeping an eye on its occupants, now unlocked it. The Inspector entered.

His first action was to search Macdonald. Finding the watch concealed on his person, he then charged Macdonald and Inez Blake with the theft. The Inspector next proceeded to make an arrest on the charge of wilful murder ...

So, whodunnit? Nicholas Blake provided eight clues to both method and motive, scattered through the text. Try to find them – and solve the mystery yourself by logical deduction, or turn to page 135 for the solution.

A Problem in White – The Solution

The Inspector arrested the Guard for the wilful murder of Arthur J. Kilmington.

Kilmington's pocket had been picked by Inez Blake, when she pretended to faint at 8.25 and his gold watch was at once passed by her to her accomplice, Macdonald.

Now Kilmington was constantly consulting his watch. It is inconceivable, if he was not killed till after 9 p.m., that he should not have missed the watch and made a scene. This point was clinched by the first-class passenger, who deposed that a man, answering to the description of Kilmington, had asked him the time at 8.50: if it had really been Kilmington, he would certainly, before inquiring the time of anyone else, have first tried to consult his own watch, found it was gone, and reported the theft. The fact that Kilmington neither reported the loss to the Guard, nor returned to his original compartment to look for the watch, proves he must have been murdered before he became aware of the loss, i.e. shortly after he left the compartment at 8.27. But the Guard claimed to have spoken to Kilmington at 9 p.m. Therefore the Guard was lying. And why should he lie, except to create an alibi for himself? This is Clue A.

The Guard claimed to have talked with Kilmington at

9 p.m. Now at 8.55 the blizzard had diminished to a light snowfall, which soon afterwards ceased. When Stansfield discovered the body, it was buried under snow. Therefore Kilmington must have been murdered while the blizzard was still raging, i.e. sometime before 9 p.m. Therefore the Guard was lying when he said Kilmington was alive at 9 p.m. This is Clue B.

Henry Stansfield, who was investigating on behalf of the Cosmopolitan Insurance Company the loss of the Countess of Axminster's emeralds, reconstructed the crime as follows:

Motive. The Guard's wife had been gravely ill before Christmas: then, just about the time of the train robbery, he had got her the best surgeon in Glasgow and put her in a nursing home (evidence of engine driver: Clue C): a Guard's pay does not usually run to such expensive treatment; it seemed likely, therefore, that the man, driven desperate by his wife's need, had agreed to take part in the robbery in return for a substantial bribe. What part did he play? During the investigation, the Guard had stated that he had left his van for five minutes, while the train was climbing the last section of Shap Bank, and on his return found the mail-bags missing. But Kilmington, who was travelling on this train, had found the Guard's van locked at this point, and now (evidence of Mrs Grant: Clue D) declared his intention of reporting the Guard. The latter knew that Kilmington's report would contradict his own evidence and thus convict him of complicity in the crime, since he had locked the van for a few minutes to throw out the mail-bags himself, and pretended to Kilmington that he had been asleep (evidence of K.) when the latter knocked at the door. So Kilmington had to be silenced.

Stansfield already had Percy Dukes under suspicion as the organiser of the robbery. During the journey, Dukes gave himself away three times. First, although it had not been mentioned in the papers, he betrayed knowledge of the point on the line where the bags had been thrown out. Second, though the loss of the emeralds had been also kept out of the Press, Dukes knew it was an emerald *necklace* which had been stolen; Stansfield had laid a trap for him by calling it a bracelet, but later in conversation Dukes referred to the 'necklace'. Third, his great discomposure at the (false) statement by Stansfield that the emeralds were worth £25,000 was the reaction of a criminal who believes he has been badly gypped by the fence to whom he has sold them.

Dukes was now planning a second train robbery, and meant to compel the Guard to act as accomplice again. Inez Blake's evidence (Clue E) of hearing him say 'You're going to help us again, chum,' etc., clearly pointed to the Guard's complicity in the previous robbery; it was almost certainly the Guard to whom she had heard Dukes say this, for only a railway servant would have known about the existence of a platelayers' hut up the line, and made an appointment to meet Dukes there; moreover, to anyone *but* a railway servant Dukes could have talked about his plans for the next robbery on the train itself, without either of them incurring suspicion should they be seen talking together.

Method. At 8.27 Kilmington goes into the Guard's van. He threatens to report the Guard, though he is quite unaware of the dire consequences this would entail for the latter. The Guard, probably on the pretext of showing him the route to the village, gets Kilmington out of the train, walks him away from the lighted area, stuns him (the bruise was a light one and did not reveal itself to Stansfield's brief examination of the body), carries him to the spot where Stansfield found the body, packs mouth and nostrils tight with snow. Then, instead of leaving well alone, the Guard decides to create an alibi for himself. He takes his victim's hat, returns to the train, puts on his own dark, off-duty overcoat, finds a solitary passenger asleep, masquerades as Kilmington inquiring the time, and strengthens the impression by saying he'd walk to the village if the relief engine did not turn up in five minutes, then returns to the body and throws down the hat beside it (Stansfield found the hat only lightly covered with snow, as compared with the body: Clue F). Moreover, the passenger noticed that the inquirer was wearing blue trousers (Clue G); the Guard's regulation suit was blue; Duke's suit was grey, Macdonald's a loud check – therefore the masquerader could not have been either of them.

The time is now 8.55. The Guard decides to reinforce his alibi by going to intercept the returning fireman. He takes a short cut from the body to the platelayers' hut. The track he now makes, compared with the beaten trail towards the village, is much more lightly filled in with snow when Stansfield finds it (Clue H); therefore it must have been made some little time after the murder, and could not incriminate Percy Dukes. The Guard meets the fireman just after 8.55.

They walk back to the train. The Guard is taken aside by Dukes, who has gone out for his 'airing', and the conversation overheard by Inez Blake takes place. The Guard tells Dukes he will meet him presently in the platelayers' hut; this is vaguely aimed to incriminate Dukes, should the murder by any chance be discovered, for Dukes would find it difficult to explain why he should have sat alone in a cold hut for half an hour just around the time when Kilmington was presumably murdered only 150 yards away.

The Guard now goes along to the engine and stays there chatting with the crew for some forty minutes. His alibi is thus established for the period from 8.55 to 9.40 p.m. His plan might well have succeeded but for three unlucky factors he could not possibly have taken into account – Stansfield's presence on the train, the blizzard stopping soon after 9 p.m., and the theft of Arthur J. Kilmington's watch.

Loopy

Ruth Rendell

At the end of the last performance, after the curtain calls,
Red Riding Hood put me on a lead and with the rest of
the company we went across to the pub. No one had taken
make-up off or changed, there was no time for that before
The George closed. I remember prancing across the road
and growling at someone on a bicycle. They loved me in
the pub – well, some of them loved me. Quite a lot were
embarrassed. The funny thing was that I should have
been embarrassed myself if I had been one of them. I
should have ignored *me* and drunk up my drink and left.
Except that it is unlikely I would have been in a pub at all.
Normally, I never went near such places. But inside the
wolf skin it was very different, everything was different
in there.

I prowled about for a while, sometimes on all fours, though this is not easy for us who are accustomed to the upright stance, sometimes loping, with my forepaws held close up to my chest. I went up to tables where people were sitting and snuffled my snout at their packets of crisps. If they were smoking I growled and waved my paws in air-clearing gestures. Lots of them were forthcoming, stroking me and making jokes or pretending terror at my red jaws and wicked little eyes. There was even one lady who took hold of my head and laid it in her lap.

Bounding up to the bar to collect my small dry sherry, I heard Bill Harkness (the First Woodcutter) say to Susan Hayes (Red Riding Hood's Mother):

'Old Colin's really come out of his shell tonight.'

And Susan, bless her, said, 'He's a real actor, isn't he?'

I was one of the few members of our company who was. I expect this is always true in amateur dramatics. There are one or two real actors, people who could have made their livings on the stage if it was not so overcrowded a profession, and the rest who just come for the fun of it and the social side. Did I ever consider the stage seriously? My father had been a civil servant, both my grandfathers in the ICS. As far back as I can remember it was taken for granted I should get my degree and go into the civil service. I never questioned it. If you have a mother like mine, one in a million, more a friend than a parent, you never feel the need to rebel. Besides, Mother gave me all the support I could have wished for in my acting. Acting as a hobby, that is. For instance, though the company made provision for hiring all the more complicated costumes for that year's Christmas pantomime, Mother made the wolf suit for me herself. It was ten times better than anything we could have hired. The head we had to buy but the body and the limbs she made from a long-haired grey fur fabric such as is manufactured for ladies' coats.

Moira used to say I enjoyed acting so much because it enabled me to lose myself and become, for a while, someone else. She said I disliked what I was and looked for ways of escape. A strange way to talk to the man you intend to marry! But before I approach the subject of Moira or, indeed, continue with this account, I should explain what its purpose is. The psychiatrist attached to this place or who visits it (I am not entirely clear which), one Dr Vernon-Peak, has asked me to write down some of my feelings and impressions. That, I said, would only be possible in the context of a narrative. Very well, he said, he had no objection. What will become of it when finished I hardly know. Will it constitute a statement to be used in court? Or will it enter Dr Vernon-Peak's files as another 'case history'? It is all the same to me. I can only tell the truth.

After The George closed, then, we took off our make-up and changed and went our several ways home.

Mother was waiting up for me. This was not invariably her habit. If I told her I should be late and to go to bed at her usual time she always did so. But I, quite naturally, was not averse to a welcome when I got home, particularly after a triumph like that one. Besides, I had been looking forward to telling her what an amusing time I had had in the pub.

Our house is late Victorian, double-fronted, of grey limestone, by no means beautiful, but a comfortable well-built place. My grandfather bought it when he retired and came home from India in 1920. Mother was ten at the time, so she has spent most of her life in that house.

Grandfather was quite a famous shot and used to go big game hunting before that kind of thing became, and rightly so, very much frowned upon. The result was that the place was full of 'trophies of the chase'. While Grandfather was alive, and he lived to a great age, we had no choice but to put up with the antlers and tusks that sprouted everywhere out of the walls, the elephant's-foot umbrella stand, and the snarling maws of *tigris* and *ursa*. We had to grin and bear it, as Mother, who has a fine turn of wit, used to put it.

But when Grandfather was at last gathered to his ancestors, reverently and without the least disrespect to him, we took down all those heads and horns and packed them away in trunks. The fur rugs, however, we did not disturb.

These days they are worth a fortune and I always felt that the tiger skins scattered across the hall parquet, the snow leopard draped across the back of the sofa and the bear into whose fur one could bury one's toes before the fire, gave to the place a luxurious look. I took off my shoes, I remember, and snuggled my toes in it that night.

Mother, of course, had been to see the show. She had come on the first night and seen me make my onslaught on Red Riding Hood, an attack so sudden and unexpected that the whole audience had jumped to its feet and gasped. (In our version we did not have the wolf actually devour Red Riding Hood. Unanimously, we agreed this would hardly have been the thing at Christmas.) Mother, however, wanted to see me wearing her creation once more, so I put it on and did some prancing and growling for her benefit. Again I noticed how curiously uninhibited I became once inside the wolf skin. For instance, I bounded up to the snow leopard and began snarling at it. I boxed at its great grey-white face and made playful bites at its ears. Down on all fours I went and pounded on the bear, fighting it, actually forcing its neck within the space of my jaws.

How Mother laughed! She said it was as good as anything in the panto and a good deal better than anything they put on television.

'Animal crackers in my soup,' she said, wiping her eyes.

'There used to be a song that went like that in my youth. How did it go on? Something about lions and tigers loop the loop.'

'Well, *lupus* means a wolf in Latin,' I said.

'And you're certainly loopy! When you put that suit on I shall have to say you're going all loopy again!'

When I put that suit on again. Did I intend to put it on again? I had not really thought about it. Yes, perhaps if I ever went to a fancy-dress party, a remote enough contingency. Yet what a shame it seemed to waste it, to pack it away like Grandfather's tusks and antlers, after all the labour Mother had put into it. That night I hung it up in my wardrobe and I remember how strange I felt when I took it off that second time, more naked than I usually felt without my clothes, almost as if I had taken off my skin.

Life kept to the 'even tenor' of its way. I felt a little flat with no rehearsals to attend and no lines to learn. Christmas came. Traditionally, Mother and I were alone on the Day itself, we would not have had it any other way, but on Boxing Day Moira arrived and Mother invited a couple of neighbours of ours as well. At some stage, I seem to recall, Susan Hayes dropped in with her husband to wish us the 'compliments of the season'.

Moira and I had been engaged for three years. We would have got married some time before, there was no question of our not being able to afford to marry, but a difficulty had arisen over where we should live. I think I may say in all fairness that the difficulty was entirely of Moira's making. No mother could have been more welcoming to a future daughter-in-law than mine. She actually wanted us to live with her at Simla House, she said we must think of it as our home and of her simply as our housekeeper. But Moira wanted us to buy a place of our own, so we had reached a deadlock, an impasse.

It was unfortunate that on that Boxing Day, after the others had gone, Moira brought the subject up again. Her brother (an estate agent) had told her of a bungalow for sale halfway between Simla House and her parents' home and it was what he called 'a real snip'. Fortunately, *I* thought, Mother managed to turn the conversation by telling us about the bungalow she and her parents had lived in in India, with its great colonnaded veranda, its English flower garden and its peepul tree. But Moira interrupted her.

'This is *our* future we're talking about, not your past. I thought Colin and I were getting married.'

Mother was quite alarmed. 'Aren't you? Surely Colin hasn't broken things off?'

'I suppose you don't consider the possibility *I* might break things off?'

Poor Mother could not help smiling at that. She smiled to cover her hurt. Moira could upset her very easily. For some reason this made Moira angry.

'I'm too old and unattractive to have any choice in the matter, is that what you mean?'

'Moira,' I said.

She took no notice. 'You may not realise it,' she said, 'but marrying me will be the making of Colin. It's what he needs to make a man of him.'

It must have slipped out before Mother quite knew what she was saying. She patted Moira's knee. 'I can quite see it may be a tough assignment, dear.'

There was no quarrel. Mother would never have allowed herself to be drawn into that. But Moira became very huffy and said she wanted to go home, so I had to get the car out and take her. All the way to her parents' house I had to listen to a catalogue of her wrongs at my hands and my mother's. By the time we parted I felt dispirited and nervous, I even wondered if I was doing the right thing, contemplating matrimony in the 'sere and yellow leaf' of forty-two.

Mother had cleared the things away and gone to bed. I went into my bedroom and began undressing. Opening the wardrobe to hang up my tweed trousers, I caught sight of the wolf suit and on some impulse I put it on.

Once inside the wolf I felt calmer and, yes, happier. I sat down in an armchair but after a while I found it more comfortable to crouch, then lie stretched out, on the floor. Lying there, basking in the warmth from the gas fire on my belly and paws, I found myself remembering tales of man's affinity with wolves, Romulus and Remus suckled by a she-wolf, the ancient myth of the werewolf, abandoned children reared by wolves even in these modern times. All this seemed to deflect my mind from the discord between Moira and my mother and I was able to go to bed reasonably happily and to sleep well.

Perhaps, then, it will not seem so strange and wonderful that the next time I felt depressed I put the suit on again. Mother was out, so I was able to have the freedom of the whole house, not just of my room. It was dusk at four but instead of putting the lights on, I prowled about the house in the twilight, sometimes catching sight of my lean grey form in the many large mirrors Mother is so fond of. Because there was so little light and our house is crammed with bulky furniture and knick-knacks, the reflection I saw looked not like a man disguised but like a real wolf that has somehow escaped and strayed into a cluttered Victorian room. Or a werewolf, that animal part of man's personality that detaches itself and wanders free while leaving behind the depleted human shape.

I crept up upon the teakwood carving of the antelope and devoured the little creature before it knew what had attacked it. I resumed my battle with the bear and we struggled in front of the fireplace, locked in a desperate hairy embrace. It was then that I heard Mother let herself in at the back door. Time had passed more quickly than I had thought. I had escaped and whisked my hind paws and tail round the bend in the stairs just before she came into the hall.

Dr Vernon-Peak seems to want to know why I began this at the age of forty-two, or rather, why I had not done it before. I wish I knew. Of course there is the simple solution that I did not have a wolf skin before, but that is not the whole answer. Was it perhaps that until then I did not know what my needs were, though partially I had satisfied them by playing the parts I was given in dramatic productions? There is one other thing. I have told him that I recall, as a very young child, having a close relationship with some large animal, a dog perhaps or a pony, though a search conducted into family history by this same assiduous Vernon-Peak has yielded no evidence that we ever kept a pet. But more of this anon.

Be that as it may, once I had lived inside the wolf, I felt the need to do so more and more. Erect on my hind legs, drawn up to my full height, I do not think I flatter myself unduly when I say I made a fine handsome animal. And having written that, I realise that I have not yet described the wolf suit, taking for granted, I suppose, that those who see this document will also see it. Yet this may not be the case. They have refused to let *me* see it, which makes me wonder if it has been cleaned and made presentable again or if it is still – but, no, there is no point in going into unsavoury details.

I have said that the body and limbs of the suit were made of long-haired grey fur fabric. The stuff of it was coarse, hardly an attractive material for a coat, I should have thought, but very closely similar to a wolf's pelt. Mother made the paws after the fashion of fur gloves but with the padded and stiffened fingers of a pair of leather gloves for the claws. The head we bought from a jokes and games shop. It had tall prick ears, small yellow eyes and a wonderful, half-open mouth, red, voracious-looking and with a double row of white fangs. The opening for me to breathe through was just beneath the lower jaw where the head joined the powerful grey hairy throat.

As the spring came I would sometimes drive out into the countryside, park the car and slip into the skin. It was far from my ambition to be seen by anyone, though. I sought solitude. Whether I should have cared for a 'beastly' companion, that is something else again. At that time I wanted merely to wander in the woods and copses or along a hedgerow in my wolf's persona. And this I did, choosing unfrequented places, avoiding anywhere that I might come in contact with the human race. I am trying, in writing this, to explain how I felt. Principally, I felt *not human*. And to be not human is to be without responsibilities and human cares. Inside the wolf, I laid aside with my humanity, my apprehensiveness about getting married, my apprehensiveness about not getting married, my fear of leaving Mother on her own, my justifiable resentment at not getting the leading part in our new production. All this got left behind with the depleted sleeping man I left behind to become a happy mindless wild creature.

Our wedding had once again been postponed. The purchase of the house Moira and I had finally agreed upon fell through at the last moment. I cannot say I was altogether sorry. It was near enough to my home, in the same street in fact as Simla House, but I had begun to wonder how I would feel passing our dear old house every day yet knowing it was not under that familiar roof I should lay my head.

Moira was very upset.

Yet, 'I won't live in the same house as your mother even for three months,' she said in answer to my suggestion. 'That's a certain recipe for disaster.'

'Mother and Daddy lived with Mother's parents for twenty years,' I said.

'Yes, and look at the result.' It was then that she made that remark about my enjoying playing parts because I disliked my real self.

There was nothing more to be said except that we must keep on house-hunting.

'We can still go to Malta, I suppose,' Moira said. 'We don't have to cancel that.'

Perhaps, but it would be no honeymoon. Anticipating the delights of matrimony was something I had not done up until then and had no intention of doing. And I was on my guard when Moira — Mother was out at her bridge evening — insisted on going up to my bedroom with me, ostensibly to check on the shade of the suit I had bought to get married in. She said she wanted to buy me a tie. Once there, she reclined on my bed, cajoling me to come and sit beside her.

I suppose it was because I was feeling depressed that I put on the wolf skin. I took off my jacket, but nothing more, of course, in front of Moira, stepped into the wolf skin, fastened it up and adjusted the head. She watched me. She had seen me in it before when she came to the pantomime.

'Why have you put that on?'

I said nothing. What could I have said? The usual contentment filled me, though, and I found myself obeying her command, loping across to the bed where she was. It seemed to come naturally to fawn on her, to rub my great prick-eared head against her breast, to enclose her hands with my paws. All kinds of fantasies filled my wolfish mind and they were of an intense piercing sweetness. If we had been on holiday then, I do not think moral resolutions would have held me back.

But unlike the lady in The George, Moira did not take

hold of my head and lay it in her lap. She jumped up and shouted at me to stop this nonsense, stop it at once, she hated it. So I did as I was told, of course I did, and got sadly out of the skin and hung it back in the cupboard. I took Moira home. On our way we called in at her brother's and looked at fresh lists of houses.

It was on one of these that we eventually settled after another month or so of picking and choosing and stalling, and we fixed our wedding for the middle of December. During the summer the company had done *Blithe Spirit* (in which I had the meagre part of Dr Bradman, Bill Harkness being Charles Condomine) and the pantomime this year was *Cinderella* with Susan Hayes in the name part and me as the Elder of the Ugly Sisters. I had calculated I should be back from my honeymoon just in time.

No doubt I would have been. No doubt I would have married and gone away on my honeymoon and come back to play my comic part had I not agreed to go shopping with Moira on her birthday. What happened that day changed everything.

It was a Thursday evening. The stores in the West End stay open late on Thursdays. We left our offices at five, met by arrangement and together walked up Bond Street. The last thing I had in view was that we should begin bickering again, though we had seemed to do little else lately. It started with my mentioning our honeymoon. We were outside Asprey's, walking along arm in arm. Since our house would not be ready for us to move into till the middle of January, I suggested we should go back for just two weeks to Simla House. We should be going there for Christmas in any case.

'I thought we'd decided to go to a hotel,' Moira said.

'Don't you think that's rather a waste of money?'

'I think,' she said in a grim sort of tone, 'I think it's money we daren't not spend,' and she drew her arm away from mine.

I asked her what on earth she meant.

'Once you get back there with Mummy you'll never move.'

I treated that with the contempt it deserved and said nothing. We walked along in silence. Then Moira began talking in a low monotone, using expressions from paperback psychology which I am glad to say I have never heard from Dr Vernon-Peak. We crossed the street and entered Selfridge's. Moira was still going on about Oedipus complexes and that nonsense about making a man of me.

'Keep your voice down,' I said. 'Everyone can hear you.'

She shouted at me to shut up, she would say what she pleased. Well, she had repeatedly told me to be a man and to assert myself, so I did just that. I went up to one of the counters, wrote her a cheque for, I must admit, a good deal more than I had originally meant to give her, put it into her hands and walked off, leaving her there.

For a while I felt not displeased with myself but on the way home in the train depression set in. I should have liked to tell Mother about it but Mother would be out, playing bridge. So I had recourse to my other source of comfort, my wolf skin. The phone rang several times while I was gambolling about the rooms but I did not answer it. I knew it was Moira. I was on the floor with Grandfather's stuffed eagle in my paws and my teeth in its neck when Mother walked in.

Bridge had ended early. One of the ladies had been taken ill and rushed to hospital. I had been too intent on my task to see the light come on or hear the door. She stood there in her old fur coat, looking at me. I let the eagle fall, I bowed my head, I wanted to die I was so ashamed and embarrassed. How little I really knew my mother! My dear faithful companion, my only friend! Might I not say, my other self?

She smiled. I could hardly believe it but she was smiling. It was that wonderful, conspiratorial, rather naughty smile of hers. 'Hallo,' she said. 'Are you going all loopy?'

In a moment she was down on her knees beside me, the fur coat enveloping her, and together we worried at the eagle, engaged in battle with the bear, attacked the ante-lope. Together we bounded into the hall to pounce upon the sleeping tigers. Mother kept laughing (and growling too) saying, what a relief, what a relief! I think we embraced. Next day when I got home she was waiting for me, transformed and ready. She had made herself an animal suit, she must have worked on it all day, out of the snow-leopard skin and a length of white fur fabric. I could see her eyes dancing through the gap in its throat.

'You don't know how I've longed to be an animal again,' she said. 'I used to be animals when you were a baby, I was a dog for a long time and then I was a bear, but your father found out and he didn't like it. I had to stop.'

So that was what I dimly remembered. I said she looked like the Queen of the Beasts.

'Do I, Loopy?' she said.

We had a wonderful weekend, Mother and I. Wolf and leopard, we breakfasted together that morning. Then we played. We played all over the house, sometimes fighting, sometimes dancing, hunting of course, carrying off our prey to the lairs we made for ourselves among the furniture. We went out in the car, drove into the country and there in a wood got into our skins and for many happy hours roamed wild among the trees.

There seemed no reason, during those two days, to become human again at all, but on the Tuesday I had a rehearsal, on the Monday morning I had to go off to work. It was coming down to earth, back to what we call reality, with a nasty bang. Still, it had its amusing side too. A lady in the train trod on my toe and I had growled at her before I remembered and turned it into a cough.

All through that weekend neither of us had bothered to answer the phone. In the office I had no choice and it was there that Moira caught me. Marriage had come to seem remote, something grotesque, something others did, not me. Animals do not marry. But that was not the sort of thing I could say to Moira. I promised to ring her, I said we must meet before the week was out.

I suppose she did tell me she would come over on the Thursday evening and show me what she had bought with the money I had given her. She knew Mother was always out on Thursdays. I suppose Moira did tell me and I failed to take it in. Nothing was important to me but being animals with Mother, Loopy and the Queen of the Beasts.

Each night as soon as I got home we made ourselves ready for our evening's games. How harmless it all was! How innocent! Like the gentle creatures in the dawn of the world before man came. Like the Garden of Eden after Adam and Eve had been sent away.

The lady who had been taken ill at the bridge evening had since died, so this week it was cancelled. But would Mother have gone anyway? Probably not. Our animal capers meant as much to her as they did to me, almost more perhaps, for she had denied herself so long. We were sitting at the dining table, eating our evening meal. Mother had cooked, I recall, a rack of lamb so that we might later gnaw the bones. We never ate it, of course, and I have since wondered what became of it. But we did begin on our soup. The bread was at my end of the table, with the bread board and the long sharp knife.

Moira, when she called and I was alone, was in the habit of letting herself in by the back door. We did not hear her, neither of us heard her, though I do remember Mother's noble head lifted a fraction before Moira came in, her fangs bared and her ears pricked. Moira opened the dining-room door and walked in. I can see her now, the complacent smile on her lips fading and the scream starting to come. She was wearing what must have been my present, a full-length white sheepskin coat.

And then? This is what Dr Vernon-Peak will particularly wish to know but what I cannot clearly remember. I remember that as the door opened I was holding the bread knife in my paws. I think I remember letting out a low growl and poising myself to spring. But what came after?

The last things I can recall before they brought me here are the blood on my fur and the two wild predatory creatures crouched on the floor over the body of the lamb.

Morse's Greatest Mystery

Colin Dexter

'Hallo!' growled Scrooge, in his accustomed voice as near as he could feign it. 'What do you mean by coming here at this time of day?'

Dickens, *A Christmas Carol*

He had knocked diffidently at Morse's North Oxford flat. Few had been invited into those book-lined, Wagner-haunted rooms: and even he – Sergeant Lewis – had never felt himself an over-welcome guest. Even at Christmas time. Not that it sounded much like the season of good-will as Morse waved Lewis inside and concluded his ill-tempered conversation with the bank manager.

'Look! If I keep a couple of hundred in my current account, that's *my* look-out. I'm not even asking for any interest on it. All I *am* asking is that you don't stick these bloody bank charges on when I go – what? once, twice a year? – into the red. It's not that I'm mean with money' – Lewis's eyebrows ascended a centimetre – 'but if you charge me again I want you to ring and tell me *why!*'

Morse banged down the receiver and sat silent.

'You don't sound as if you've caught much of the Christmas spirit,' ventured Lewis.

'I don't like Christmas – never have.'

'You staying in Oxford, sir?'

'I'm going to decorate.'

'What – decorate the Christmas cake?'

'Decorate the kitchen. I don't like Christmas cake – never did.'

'You sound more like Scrooge every minute, sir.'

'*And* I shall read a Dickens novel. I always do over Christmas. Re-read, rather.'

'If I were just *starting* on Dickens, which one—?'

'I'd put *Bleak House* first, *Little Dorrit* second—'

The phone rang and Morse's secretary at HQ informed him that he'd won a £50 gift-token in the Police Charity Raffle, and this time Morse cradled the receiver with considerably better grace.

'"Scrooge", did you say, Lewis? I'll have you know I bought five tickets – a quid apiece! – in that Charity Raffle.'

'I bought five tickets myself, sir.'

Morse smiled complacently. 'Let's be more charitable, Lewis! It's *supporting* these causes that's important, not *winning*.'

'I'll be in the car, sir,' said Lewis quietly. In truth, he was beginning to feel irritated. Morse's irascibility he could stomach; but he couldn't stick hearing much more about Morse's selfless generosity!

Morse's old Jaguar was in dock again ('Too mean to buy a new one!' his colleagues claimed) and it was Lewis's job that day to ferry the chief inspector around; doubtless, too (if things went to form), to treat him to the odd pint or two. Which indeed appeared a fair probability, since Morse had so managed things on that Tuesday morning that their arrival at the George would coincide with opening time. As they drove out past the railway station, Lewis told Morse what he'd managed to discover about the previous day's events ...

The patrons of the George had amassed £400 in aid of the Littlemore Charity for Mentally Handicapped Children, and this splendid total was to be presented to the Charity's Secretary at the end of the week, with a photographer promised from *The Oxford Times* to record the grand occasion. Mrs Michaels, the landlady, had been dropped off at the bank in Carfax by her husband at about 10.30 a.m., and had there exchanged a motley assemblage of coins and notes for forty brand-new tenners.

After this she had bought several items (including grapes for a daughter just admitted to hospital) before catching a minibus back home, where she had arrived just after midday. The money, in a long white envelope, was in her shopping bag, together with her morning's purchases. Her husband had not yet returned from the Cash and Carry Stores, and on re-entering the George via the saloon bar, Mrs Michaels had heard the telephone ringing. Thinking that it was probably the hospital (it was) she had dumped her bag on the bar counter and rushed to answer it. On her return, the envelope was gone.

At the time of the theft, there had been about thirty people in the saloon bar, including the regular OAPs, the usual cohort of pool-playing unemployables, and a pre-Christmas party from a local firm. And – yes! – from the very beginning Lewis had known that the chances of recovering the money were virtually nil. Even so, the three perfunctory interviews that Morse conducted appeared to Lewis to be sadly unsatisfactory.

After listening a while to the landlord's unilluminating testimony, Morse asked him why it had taken him so long to conduct his business at the Cash and Carry; and although the explanation given seemed perfectly adequate, Morse's dismissal of this first witness had seemed almost offensively abrupt. And no man could have been more quickly or more effectively antagonised than the temporary barman (on duty the previous morning) who refused to answer Morse's brusque enquiry about the present state of his overdraft. What then of the attractive, auburn-haired Mrs Michaels? After a rather lop-sided smile had introduced Morse to her regular if slightly nicotine-stained teeth, that distressed lady had been unable to fight back her tears as she sought to explain to Morse why she'd insisted on some genuine notes for the publicity photographer instead of a phonily magnified cheque.

But wait! Something dramatic had just happened to Morse, Lewis could see that: as if the light had suddenly shined upon a man that hitherto had sat in darkness. He (Morse) now asked – amazingly! – whether by any chance the good lady possessed a pair of bright green, high-heeled leather shoes; and when she replied that, yes, she did, Morse smiled serenely, as though he had solved the secret of the universe, and promptly summoned into the lounge bar not only the three he'd just interviewed but all those now in the George who had been drinking there the previous morning.

As they waited, Morse asked for the serial numbers of the stolen notes, and Lewis passed over a scrap of paper on which some figures had been hastily scribbled in blotchy Biro. 'For Christ's sake, man!' hissed Morse. 'Didn't they teach you to write at school?'

Lewis breathed heavily, counted to five, and then

painstakingly rewrote the numbers on a virginal piece of paper: 773741–773780. At which numbers Morse glanced cursorily before sticking the paper in his pocket, and proceeding to address the George's regulars.

He was *virtually* certain (he said) of who had stolen the money. What he was *absolutely* sure about was exactly where that money was *at that very moment*. He had the serial numbers of the notes – but that was of no importance whatsoever now. The thief might well have been tempted to spend the money earlier – but not any more! And why not? Because at this Christmas time that person *no longer had the power to resist his better self*.

In that bar, stilled now and silent as the grave itself, the faces of Morse's audience seemed mesmerised – and remained so as Morse gave his instructions that the notes should be replaced in their original envelope and returned (he cared not by what means) to Sergeant Lewis's office at Thames Valley Police HQ *within the next twenty-four hours*.

As they drove back, Lewis could restrain his curiosity no longer. 'You really are confident that——?'

'Of course!'

'I never seem to be able to put the clues together myself, sir.'

'Clues? What clues, Lewis? I didn't know we had any.'

'Well, those shoes, for example. How do they fit in?'

'Who said they fitted in anywhere? It's just that I used to know an auburn-haired beauty who had six – *six*, Lewis! – pairs of bright green shoes. They suited her, she said.'

'So ... they've got nothing to do with the case at all?'

'Not so far as I know,' muttered Morse.

The next morning a white envelope was delivered to Lewis's office, though no one at reception could recall when or whence it had arrived. Lewis immediately rang Morse to congratulate him on the happy outcome of the case.

'There's just one thing, sir. I'd kept that scrappy bit of paper with the serial numbers on it, and these are brand-new notes all right – but they're not the same ones!'

'Really?' Morse sounded supremely unconcerned.

'You're not worried about it?'

'Good Lord, no! You just get that money back to ginger-knob at the George, and tell her to settle for a jumbo-cheque next time! Oh, and one other thing, Lewis. I'm on *leave*. So no interruptions from anybody – understand?'

'Yes, sir. And, er ... Happy Christmas, sir!'

'And to you, old friend!' replied Morse quietly.

The bank manager rang just before lunch that same day. 'It's about the four hundred pounds you withdrew yesterday, Inspector. I did promise to ring about any further bank charges—'

'I explained to the girl,' protested Morse. 'I needed the money quickly.'

'Oh, it's perfectly all right. But you did say you'd call in this morning to transfer—'

'Tomorrow! I'm up a ladder with a paint brush at the moment.'

Morse put down the receiver and again sank back in the armchair with the crossword. But his mind was far away, and some of the words he himself had spoken kept echoing around his brain: something about one's better self … And he smiled, for he knew that this would be a Christmas he might enjoy almost as much as the children up at Littlemore, perhaps. He had solved so many mysteries in his life. Was he now, he wondered, beginning to glimpse the solution to the greatest mystery of them all?

The Jar of Ginger

Gladys Mitchell

'But you would have to be certain,' said Jaffrick, 'that the person you wanted to murder would eat the whole lot. I mean, look at the risk otherwise. Why, you might even eat the wrong piece yourself.'

We were young then. We called ourselves *The Society of Thugs* and the only rule for admission to membership was that you should describe to the club a method for murdering your nearest and dearest. We interpreted this heading widely. It could be held that *nearest* and *dearest* need not be synonymous terms. For instance, Withers had given a perfectly good and very interesting account of how he could murder his landlady, and P. J. Smith had described a method for murdering himself. In the one case the operative word was *nearest* and in the other case

dearest, P. J. Smith holding (against no particular oppos-
ition) that he was the dearest person known to himself.
For one thing he contended that he was of more expense
to himself than anybody else was (he was a bachelor, of
course), and he confessed also that he preferred himself
and his own company even to us and ours.

It was a man called Chart who had drawn the remark
from Jaffrick. Chart was not known personally to any
of us. He had rolled up in company with Bellew, but
Bellew had only run into him that evening in a bar, and
as Chart (admittedly slightly stewed when they arrived)
had stood him a drink because he said he liked his face,
Bellew had brought him along after telling him the terms
of membership.

He was a good deal older than the rest of us. Forty-
five, I should say, and his story of how he could murder
his wife was interesting enough in a sense, but, as Jaffrick
argued, the method he described could not be guaranteed
to work. The risk to the murderer was as great as to the
intended victim.

'Ah, but after a time you wouldn't put the *whole* jar of
ginger on the table,' said Chart. 'Perhaps I ought to make
that bit a little clearer. By the way, my wife is dead, so
my choice of her as my victim no longer has any real significance. I shouldn't like you gentlemen to think that my
selection of somebody I could murder was in questionable

taste. Yes, well, you see, you'd buy the pot of ginger ... one of those handsome, decorated, Chinese things, you know – as a present for the house around Christmas time. You'd buy the biggest and most beautiful pot you could afford, because the more ginger you had to play about with, the easier your task would be and the greater its chance of success.

'Well, at first you would dig for your ginger, and the wife would dig for hers. This would go on for quite some time, the ginger, of course, innocent stuff, gradually getting lower and the action of digging for it stickier.

'One point that I must emphasise is that for the successful carrying out of your plan you would need to keep the pot of ginger firmly under your own control. This could be done by insisting, with humorous gallantry, that you always place it upon the table yourself.

'"No, it's *my* present to the house," you would laughingly say, looking at it affectionately as it stood in its celestial glory on the sideboard. "Nobody else need even dust it! I'll see to all that!" Of course, if you had any sense, you wouldn't make it the first present to the house that you had ever bought. If one proposes to murder one's nearest and dearest, one leads up to it by degrees. Even three years is not too long to wait. There is no point in bungling the job, let alone spoiling the ship for a ha'porth of tar.

'Well, when the ginger in the jar was low enough to

make spearing it out a messy, sticky business, you would introduce your next little move. You would bring home a very small, expensive, cut-glass dish … something about the size of a domestic ash-tray. In fact, a really lovely ash-tray about three to four inches across would do as well as anything else.

'"Look, darling," you would say. "For our lovely ginger! And when we've finished the ginger we've got a perfectly good ash-tray. My next present to the house had better be some super-Turkish or Egyptian."'

'But I can't see a woman swallowing all this, you know,' said Jaffrick. 'I mean, by the time you'd got to this stage you'd have had disagreements and a good many quarrels. I mean, she would tend to suspect your *bona fides* and so forth, wouldn't she?'

'That would depend upon how much you hated her,' replied Chart. 'If it was only the ordinary give and take of the average married couple, she would naturally suspect your good intentions. She would take it for granted that you were covering up some peccadillo of your own by bringing back presents for the house. But a real, honest, devilish, implacable hatred, that's quite a different matter. You would disguise that as long as ever you could, because you would know that sooner or later it would mean either murder or divorce, and divorce is so confoundedly expensive.'

We all gloomily agreed. We were young, as I said, and all bachelors. It takes a bachelor to be ideally (as it were) gloomy and profound about marriage.

'Go on about the ginger,' said Bellew, for our guest showed signs of dropping off to sleep. 'The trouble, as I see it, would not be to disguise your hatred – any competent hater could do that! – but to make perfectly certain, ash-tray or no ash-tray, that you didn't pick the wrong piece of ginger yourself.'

'Simplicity itself,' said P. J. Smith. 'You'd stick a pin in the poisoned lump and then chew carefully.'

We all disputed this, an ordinarily silent bloke called Carruthers and myself holding that the danger of swallowing or being pricked by the pin would be almost equal to the danger of swallowing the lethal dose in the piece of ginger, and, further, that if the victim struck on the pin she would throw the rest of the ginger away.

'Pins!' said P. J. Smith. 'Oh no! Who on earth worries about pins? Stuck them deeply into chaps at school, and chaps at school stuck them deeply into me. Nothing to it. Nobody cares about pins!'

Carruthers and I said that we did, and the pin and anti-pin argument lasted the club for half an hour and tended to embrace such subjects as canteen meals and the recent bus strike. It then passed lightly over films, the scenery around the Matterhorn and yachting on the Norfolk

Broads. In fact, Rowbotham, our president, had to call the meeting to order.

'Will somebody move,' he said plaintively, 'that the prospective candidate be allowed to continue his exposition?'

Half a dozen of us who were losing the argument immediately accommodated him, and Chart resumed his remarks.

'You see,' he said, when we had woken him up, 'one would only put out four pieces of ginger each time on the small glass dish.'

'Three-to-one chance,' said Bellew.

'Granted,' said Chart, 'and your remarks about pins have interested me deeply. Nevertheless, there would be one infallible rule. You yourself would always choose your piece of ginger first. This would reduce the odds, of course, but, in my view, unnecessarily. There would always be a slight element of chance or risk, but the wise man would slice off the end of the noxious piece of ginger so that he could recognise it. The technique is really very simple. One would spear an innocuous piece of ginger, leaving three other pieces on the dish. It might be that the party of the second part would pick the piece with the strychnine in it straight away. If not, there would be only two pieces left, and a wise murderer would give his victim the choice of these, and not attempt to encourage her to eat both.'

'I can't see that,' said Bellew. P. J. Smith said that of

course he could. If the victim picked the non-poisonous piece it would be simplicity itself to say that one did not want anymore and leave it at that. Other members disputed this. It would look very fishy, they said, to leave a piece on the dish if one was not in the habit of doing this. And what of the ill-manners of helping oneself first? they enquired.

Chart, looking crestfallen, agreed.

'Besides, what would you do with the fatal piece?' asked Bellew, pressing home his advantage. 'You could hardly put it back into the jar, and you'd not want to throw it away and doctor up another piece, would you?'

P. J. Smith argued that to throw it away would be the only thing to do. He contended, however, that as strychnine is not readily purchasable, one would have to hope for the best. One could not go on indefinitely impregnating pieces of ginger with poison in the hope that at some point the intended victim would choose the right chunk and consume it.

'There's the mathematical odds to consider,' said Carruthers. 'The permutations and combinations even of so small a number as four must be quite exhilarating.'

As he was an accountant by profession, we gave him best over that.

'But do go on, Mr Chart,' said Bellew. 'After all, this is your story, and, so far, I'm bound to tell you that you have my vote of membership. I don't think your scheme would work, but there are possibilities in it.'

Chart said that he was obliged to him, and the rest of us politely applauded.

'You see,' he said, 'actually it's quite easy. A person who likes ginger in syrup would be fond of mango chutney. One would, therefore, slip the poisoned piece of ginger into the mango chutney, where it would be inconspicuous, I think, and when the chutney came on the table one would avoid that particular piece. Sooner or later, surely, the intended victim would be bound to choose it, and – hey presto! – one would be a widower without trouble or risk.'

'I don't know about risk,' said a man named Denison. 'The symptoms of poisoning by strychnine are rather obvious, aren't they?'

'But it need not be strychnine,' said P. J. Smith. 'A lethal quantity of arsenic would be just as good, and the symptoms of arsenical poisoning are not easily distinguished from those of acute indigestion. I move that we accept Mr Chart's account, substituting arsenic for strychnine.'

We all voted in favour of this amendment except Carruthers, who said that the introduction of a piece of China ginger into a mango chutney would arouse doubt and suspicion in the mind of the intended victim. In mango chutney, he contended, one did not expect to find any kind of ginger but the long, narrow, hairy kind, unsweetened and as hot as hell, which forms part of the contents of any respectable jar.

This statement called for more beer and considerably more argument. As it was getting late, even for us, Bellew suggested that Mr Chart be allowed to conclude his exposition, as the caretaker would be wanting to close the premises. We did not pay enough rent, he pointed out, to be in a position to take too many liberties.

This seemed common sense. Chart begged our pardon (rather thickly) for keeping us out of bed, and said that really he had finished what he had to say. We began to collect the tankards and glasses, but P. J. Smith said that he would like to ask the new member a question.

'I can see,' he said, 'that ginger, either in syrup or in a chutney, would be almost a perfect vehicle for poison, but what if the subject didn't like it?'

'Oh, but she did,' said Chart. 'She absolutely loved it, don't you see.'

Rumpole and the
Old Familiar Faces

John Mortimer

In the varied ups and downs, the thrills and spills in the
life of an Old Bailey hack, one thing stands as stone. Your
ex-customers will never want to see you again. Even if
you've steered them through the rocks of the prosecution case and brought them out to the calm waters of a
not guilty verdict, they won't plan further meetings, host
reunion dinners, or even send you a card on your birthday. If they catch a glimpse of you on the Underground,
or across a crowded wine bar, they will bury their faces in
their newspapers or look studiously in the opposite direction. This is understandable. Days in court probably
represent a period of time they'd rather forget and, as a

rule, I'm not especially keen to renew an old acquaintance when a face I once saw in the Old Bailey dock reappears at a 'Scales of Justice' dinner or at the Inns of Court garden party. Reminiscences of the past are best avoided, and what is required is a quick look and a quiet turn away. There have been times, however, when recognising a face seen in trouble has greatly assisted me in the solution of some legal problem and carried me to triumph in a difficult case. Such occasions have been rare but, like number thirteen buses, two of them turned up in short order around a Christmas which I remember as being one of the oddest, but certainly the most rewarding, I ever spent.

* * *

'A traditional British pantomime. There's nothing to beat it!'

'You go to the pantomime, Rumpole?' Claude asked with unexpected interest.

'I did when I was a boy. It made a lasting impression on me.'

'Pantomime?' The American judge who was our fellow guest around the Erskine-Brown dinner table was clearly a stranger to such delights. 'Is that some kind of mime show? Lots of feeling imaginary walls and no one saying anything?'

'Not at all. You take some good old story, like *Robin Hood* ...'

'Robin Hood's the star?'

'Well, yes. He's played by some strapping girl who slaps her thighs and says lines like, "Cheer up, Babes in the Wood, Robin's not far away."'

'You mean there's cross-dressing?' The American visitor was puzzled.

'Well, if you want to call it that. And Robin's mother is played by a red-nosed comic.'

'A female comic?'

'No. A male one.'

'That sounds interesting,' he said in a tone that suggested he had the wrong idea. 'We have clubs for that sort of thing in Pittsburgh.'

'It's not what you're thinking,' I assured him. 'The dame's a comic character who gets the audience singing.'

'Singing?'

'The words come down on a sort of giant song sheet,' I explained, 'and she, who is really a he, gets the audience to sing along.'

Emboldened by Erskine-Brown's claret (smoother on the tongue but with less of a kick than Château Thames Embankment), I broke into a stanza of the song I was introduced to by Robin Hood's masculine mother.

I may be just a nipper,
But I've always loved a kipper ...
And so does my loving wife.
If you've got a girl, just slip her
A loving golden kipper
And she'll be yours for life.

'Is that all?' The transatlantic judge still seemed puzzled.

'All I can remember.'

'I think you're wrong, Mr Rumpole.'

'What?'

'I think you're wrong and those lines do indeed have some significance along the lines I suggested.' And the judge fell silent, contemplating the unusual acts suggested.

'I see they're doing *Aladdin* at the Tufnell Park Empire. Do you think the twins might enjoy it, Rumpole?'

The speaker was Mrs Justice Erskine-Brown (Phillida Trant as she was in happier days when I called her the Portia of our chambers), still possessed of a beauty that would break the hearts of the toughest prosecutors and make old lags swoon with lust even as she passed a stiff custodial sentence. The twins she spoke of were Tristan and Isolde, so named by her opera-loving husband Claude, who was now bending Hilda's ear on the subject of Covent Garden's latest *Ring* cycle.

'I think the twins would adore it. Just the thing to cure

the Wagnerian death wish and bring them into a world of sanity.'

'Sanity?' The visiting judge sounded doubtful. 'With old guys dressed up as mothers?'

'I promise you, they'll love every minute of it.' And then I made another promise that sounded rash even as I spoke the words. 'I know I would. I'll take them myself.'

'Thank you, Rumpole.' Phillida spoke in her gentlest judicial voice, but I knew my fate was sealed. 'We'll keep you to that.'

'It'll have to be after Christmas,' Hilda said. We've been invited up to Norfolk for the holiday.'

As she said the word 'Norfolk' a cold, sweeping wind seemed to cut through the central heating of the Erskine-Browns' Islington dining room and I felt a warning shiver.

I have no rooted objection to Christmas Day, but I must say it's an occasion when time tends to hang particularly heavily on the hands. From the early morning alarm call of carols piping on Radio 4 to the closing headlines and a restless, liverish sleep, the day can seem as long as a fraud on the Post Office tried before Mr Injustice Graves.

It takes less than no time for me to unwrap the tie which I will seldom wear, and for Hilda to receive the annual bottle of lavender water which she lays down rather than puts to immediate use. The highlights after that are the Queen's Speech, when I lay bets with myself as to whether Hilda will stand to attention when the television plays the National Anthem, and the thawed-out Safeway bird followed by port (an annual gift from my faithful solicitor Bonny Bernard) and pudding. I suppose what I have against Christmas Day is that the courts are all shut and no one is being tried for anything.

That Christmas, Hilda had decided on a complete change of routine. She announced it in a circuitous fashion by saying, one late November evening, 'I was at school with Poppy Longstaff.'

'What's that got to do with it?' I knew the answer to this question, of course. Hilda's old school has this in common with polar expeditions, natural disasters and the last war; those who have lived through it are bound together for life and can always call on each other for mutual assistance.

'Poppy's Eric is Rector of Coldsands. And for some reason or other he seems to want to meet you, Rumpole.'

'Meet me?'

'That's what she said.'

'So does that mean I have to spend Christmas in the Arctic Circle and miss our festivities?'

'It's not the Arctic Circle. It's Norfolk, Rumpole. And our festivities aren't all that festive. So, yes. You have to go.' It was a judgement for which there was no possible appeal.

My first impression of Coldsands was a gaunt church tower, presumably of great age, pointing an accusing finger to heaven from a cluster of houses on the edge of a sullen, gunmetal sea. My second was one of intense cold. As soon as we got out of the taxi, we were slapped around the face by a wind which must have started in freezing Siberia and gained nothing in the way of warmth on its journey across the plains of Europe.

'In the bleak midwinter / Frosty wind made moan ...' wrote that sad old darling Christina Rossetti. Frosty winds made considerable moan round the rectory at Coldsands, owing to the doors that stopped about an inch short of the stone floors and the windows which never shut properly, causing the curtains to billow like the sails of a ship at sea.

We were greeted cheerfully by Poppy. Hilda's friend had one of those round, childishly pretty faces often seen on seriously fat women. She seemed to keep going on incessant cups of hot, sweet tea and a number of cardigans. If she moved like an enormous tent, her husband Eric was a slender wraith of a man with a high aquiline nose, two flapping wings of grey hair on each side of his face, and a vague air of perpetual anxiety broken, now and then, by high and unexpected laughter. He made cruciform gestures, as though remembering the rubric 'spectacles, testicles, wallet and watch' and forgetting where these important articles were kept.

'Eric,' his wife explained, 'is having terrible trouble with the church tower.'

'Oh, dear.' Hilda shot me a look of stern disapproval, which I knew meant that it would be more polite if I abandoned my overcoat while tea was being served. 'How worrying for you, Eric.'

The Reverend Eric went into a long, excited and high-pitched speech. The gist of it was that the tower, although of rare beauty, had not been much restored since the Saxons built it and the Normans added the finishing touches. Fifty thousand pounds was needed for essential repairs, and the thermometer, erected outside the church for the appeal, was stuck at one hundred and twenty pounds – the proceeds from an emergency jumble sale.

'You particularly wanted Horace to come this Christmas?' Hilda asked the Man of God with the air of someone anxious to solve a baffling mystery. 'I wonder why that was?'

'Yes. I wonder!' Eric looked startled. 'I wonder why on earth I wanted to ask Horace. I don't believe he's got fifty thousand smackers in his back pocket!' At this, he shook with laughter.

'There,' I told him. 'Your lack of faith is entirely justified.' I wasn't exactly enjoying Coldsands Rectory, so I was a little miffed that the Reverend couldn't remember why he'd asked me there in the first place.

'We had hoped that Donald Compton would help us out,' Poppy told us. 'I mean, he wouldn't notice fifty thousand. But he took exception to what Eric said at the Remembrance Day service.'

'Armistice Day in the village.' Eric's grey wings of hair trembled as he nodded in delighted affirmation. 'And I prayed for dead German soldiers. It seemed only fair.'

'Fair perhaps, darling. But hardly tactful,' his wife told him. 'Donald Compton thought it was distinctly unpatriotic. He's bought the Old Manor House,' she explained to Hilda. From then on the conversation turned exclusively to this Compton and was carried on in the tones of awe and muted wonder with which people always talk about the very rich. Compton, it seemed, after a difficult start in England, had gone to Canada where, during a ten-year stay, he had laid the foundations of his fortune. His much younger wife was quite charming, probably Canadian, and not in the least stand-offish. He had built the village hall, the cricket pavilion and a tennis court for the school. Only Eric's unfortunate sympathy for the German dead had caused Compton's bounty to stop short at the church tower.

'I've done hours of hard knee-work,' the rector told us, 'begging the Lord to soften Mr Compton's heart towards our tower. No result so far, I fear.'

Apart from this one lapse, the charming Donald

Compton seemed to be the perfect English squire and country gent. I would see him in church on Christmas morning, and we had also been invited for drinks before lunch at the manor. The Reverend Eric and the smiling Poppy made it sound as though the Pope and the Archbishop of Canterbury would be out with the carol singers and we'd been invited to drop in for high tea at Windsor Castle. I prayed for a yule log blazing at the manor so that I could, in the true spirit of Christmas, thaw out gradually.

'Now, as a sign of Christmas fellowship, will you all stand and shake hands with those in front of and behind you?' Eric, in full canonicals, standing on the steps in front of the altar, made this suggestion as though he had just thought of the idea. I stood reluctantly. I had found myself a place in the church near a huge, friendly, gently humming, occasionally belching radiator and I was clinging to it and stroking it as though it were a new-found mistress (not that I have much experience of new- or even old-found mistresses). The man who turned to me from the front row seemed to be equally reluctant. He was, as Hilda had pointed out excitedly, the great Donald Compton in person – a man of middle height with silver hair, dressed in a tweed suit, and with a tan which it must have been expensive to preserve during winter. He had soft brown eyes which looked away from me almost at once as, with a touch of dry fingers, he was gone and I was left, for the rest of the service, with no more than a well-tailored back and the sound of an uncertain tenor voice joining in the hymns.

I turned to the row behind to shake hands with an elderly woman who had madness in her eyes and whispered conspiratorially to me, 'You cold, dear? Like to borrow my gloves? We're used to a bit of chill weather round these parts.' I declined politely and went back to hugging the radiator, and as I did so a sort of happiness stole over me. To start with, the church was beautiful, with a high timbered roof and walls of weathered stone, peppered with marble tributes to dead inhabitants of the manor. It was decorated with holly and mistletoe. A tree glowed and there were candles over a crib. I thought how many generations of Coldsands villagers, their eyes bright and faces flushed with the wind, had belted out these hymns. I also thought how depressed the great Donald Compton – who had put on little gold half-glasses to read the prophecy from Isaiah: 'For unto us a child is born, unto us a son is given: and the government shall be upon his shoulder: and his name shall be called Wonderful' – would feel if Jesus' instruction to sell all and give it to the poor should ever be taken literally.

And then I wondered why it was that, as he had touched

my fingers and turned away, I had felt that I had lived through that precise moment before.

There was, as it turned out, a huge log fire crackling at the manor, throwing a dancing light on the marble floor of the circular entrance hall with its great staircase leading up into private shadows. The cream of Coldsands was being entertained with champagne and canapés by the new Lord of the Manor. The decibels rose as the champagne went down and the little group began to sound like an army of tourists in the Sistine Chapel – noisy, excited and wonderstruck.

'They must all be his ancestors.' Hilda was looking at the pictures on the walls and, in particular, at a general in a scarlet coat, on a horse prancing at the front of some distant battle.

My mouth was full of cream cheese enveloped in smoked salmon. I swallowed it and said, 'Oh, I shouldn't think so. After all, he only bought the house recently.'

'But I expect he brought his family portraits here from somewhere else.'

'You mean, he had them under the bed in his old bachelor flat in Wimbledon and now he's hung them round an acre or two of walls?'

'Do try and be serious, Rumpole. You're not nearly as funny as you think you are. Just look at the family resemblance. I'm absolutely certain that all of these are old Comptons.' And it was when she said this that I remembered everything perfectly clearly.

He was with his wife. She was wearing a black velvet dress and had long, golden hair that sparkled in the firelight. They were talking to a bald, pink-faced man and his short and dumpy wife, and they were all laughing. Compton's laughter stopped as he saw me coming towards him. He said, 'I don't think we've met.'

'Yes,' I replied. 'We shook hands briefly in church this morning. My name's Rumpole and I'm staying with the Longstaffs. But didn't we meet somewhere else?'

'Good old Eric! We have our differences, of course, but he's a saintly man. This is my wife Lorelei, and Colonel and Maudy Jacobs. I expect you'd like to see the library, wouldn't you, Rumpole? I'm sure you're interested in ancient history. Will you all excuse us?'

It was two words from Hilda that had done it – 'old' and 'Compton'. I knew then what I should have remembered when we had touched hands in the pews, that Old Compton is a street in Soho, and that this was perhaps why Riccardo (known as Dicko) Perducci had adopted the name. I had received that very same handshake – a slight touch and a quick turn away – when I had said goodbye to him in the cells under the Old Bailey and left him to start seven years for blackmail. The trial had ended, I now remembered, just before a long-distant Christmas.

The Perducci territory had been, in those days, not rolling Norfolk acres but a number of Soho strip clubs and clip joints. Girls would stand in front of these last-named resorts and lure the lonely, the desperate and the unwary in. Sometimes they would escape after paying twenty pounds for a watery cocktail. Unlucky, affluent and important customers might get even more, carefully recorded by microphones and cameras to produce material which was used for systematic and highly profitable blackmail. The victim in Dicko's case was an obscure and not much loved circuit judge, so it was regarded as particularly serious by the prosecuting authority.

When I mitigated for Dicko, I stressed the lack of direct evidence against him. He was a shadowy figure who kept himself well in the background and was known as a legend rather than a familiar face around Soho. 'That only shows what a big wheel he is,' Judge Bullingham, who was unfortunately trying the case, bellowed unsympathetically. In desperation I tried the Christmas approach on him. 'Crimes forgiven, sins remitted, mercy triumphant, such was the message of the story that began in Bethlehem,' I told the court, at which the Mad Bull snorted that, as far as he could remember, that story had ended in a criminal trial and a stiff sentence for at least one thief.

'I suppose something like this was going to happen sooner or later.' We were standing in the library in front of a comforting fire, among leather-bound books which I strongly suspected had been bought by the yard. The new, like the old, Dicko was soft-eyed, quietly spoken, almost unnaturally calm – the perfect man behind the scenes of a blackmailing operation or a country estate.

'Not necessarily,' I told him. 'It's just that my wife has many old school friends and Poppy Longstaff is one of them. Well now, you seem to have done pretty well for yourself. Solid citizens still misconducting themselves around Old Compton Street, are they?'

'I wouldn't know. I gave all that up and went into the property business.'

'Really? Where did you do that? Canada?'

'I never saw Canada.' He shook his head. 'Garwick Prison. Up-and-coming area in the Home Counties. The screws there were ready and willing to do the deals on the outside. I paid them embarrassingly small commissions.'

'How long were you there?'

'Four years. By the time I came out I'd got my first million.'

'Well, then, I did you a good turn, losing your case. A bit of luck His Honour Judge Bullingham didn't believe in the remission of sins.'

'You think I got what I deserved?'

I stretched my hands to the fire. I could hear the cocktail chatter from the marble hall of the eighteenth-century manor. 'Use every man after his desert, and who should 'scape whipping?' I quoted *Hamlet* at him.

'Then I can trust you, Rumpole? The Lord Chancellor's going to put me on the local bench.'

'The Lord Chancellor lives in a world of his own.'

'You don't think I'd do well as a magistrate?'

'I suppose you'd speak from personal experience of crime. And have some respect for the quality of mercy.'

'I've got no time for that, Rumpole.' His voice became quieter but harder. The brown eyes lost their softness. That, I thought, was how he must have looked when one of his clip joint girls was caught with the punters' cash stuffed in her tights. 'It's about time we cracked down on crime. Well, now, I can trust you not to go out there and spread the word about the last time we met?'

'That depends.'

'On what?'

'How well you have understood the Christmas message.'

'Which is?'

'Perhaps, generosity.'

'I see. So you want your bung?'

'Oh, not me, Dicko. I've been paid, inadequately, by Legal Aid. But there's an impoverished church tower in urgent need of resuscitation.'

'That Eric Longstaff, our rector – he's not a patriot!'

'And are you?'

'I do a good deal of work locally for the British Legion.'

'And, I'm sure, next Poppy Day they'll appreciate what you've done for the church tower.'

He looked at me for a long minute in silence, and I thought that if this scene had been taking place in a back room in Soho there might, quite soon, have been the flash of a knife. Instead, his hand went to an inside pocket and produced nothing more lethal than a chequebook.

'While you're in a giving mood,' I said, 'the rectory's in desperate need of central heating.'

'This is bloody blackmail!' Dicko Perducci, now known as Donald Compton, said.

'Well,' I told him, 'you should know.'

Christmas was over. The year turned, stirred itself and opened its eyes on a bleak January. Crimes were committed, arrests were made, and the courtrooms were filled, once again, with the sounds of argument. I went down to the Old Bailey on a trifling matter of fixing the date of a trial before Mrs Justice Erskine-Brown. As I was leaving, the usher came and told me that the judge wanted to see me in her private room on a matter of urgency.

Such summonses always fill me with apprehension and a vague feeling of guilt. What had I done? Got the date of the trial hopelessly muddled? Addressed the court with my trousers carelessly unzipped? I was relieved when the learned Phillida greeted me warmly and even offered me a glass of sherry, poured from her own personal decanter. 'It was so kind of you to offer, Rumpole,' she said unexpectedly.

'Offer what?' I was puzzled.

'You told us how much you adored the traditional British pantomime.'

'So I did.' For a happy moment I imagined Her Ladyship as Principal Boy, her shapely legs encased in black tights, her neat little wig slightly askew, slapping her thigh and calling out, in bell-like tones, 'Cheer up, Rumpole, Portia's not far away.'

'The twins are looking forward to it enormously.'

'Looking forward to what?'

'*Aladdin* at the Tufnell Park Empire. I've got tickets for the nineteenth of January. You do remember promising to take them, don't you?'

'Well, of course.' What else might I have said after the fifth glass of Erskine-Brown St Emilion? 'I'd love to be of the party. And will old Claude be buying us a dinner afterwards?'

'I really don't think you should go around calling people "old", Rumpole.' Phillida now looked miffed, and I downed the sherry before she took it into her head to deprive me of it. 'Claude's got us tickets for Pavarotti – *L'Elisir d'Amore.* You might buy the children a burger after the show. Oh, and it's not far from us on the Tube. It really was sweet of you to invite them.' At which she smiled at me and refilled my glass in a way which made it clear she was not prepared to hear further argument.

It all turned out better than I could have hoped. Tristan and Isolde, unlike their Wagnerian namesakes, were cheerful, reasonably polite, and only seemed anxious to disassociate themselves, as far as possible, from the old fart who was escorting them. At every available opportunity they would touch me for cash and then scamper off to buy ice cream, chocolates, sandwiches or Sprite. I was left in reasonable peace to enjoy the performance.

And enjoy it I did. Aladdin was a personable young woman with an upturned nose, a voice which could have been used to wake up patients coming round from their anaesthesia, and memorable thighs. Uncle Abanazer was played, Isolde told me, by an actor who portrayed a social worker with domestic problems in a long-running television series. Wishy and Washy did sing to electric guitars (deafeningly amplified) but Widow Twankey, played by a certain Jim Diamond, was all a dame should be – a nimble little cockney, fitted up with a sizeable false bosom, a flaming red wig, sweeping eyelashes and scarlet lips. Never have I heard the immortal line, 'Where's that naughty boy Aladdin got to?' better delivered. I joined in loudly (Tristan and Isolde sat silent and embarrassed) when the Widow and Aladdin conducted us in the singing of 'Please Don't Pinch My Tomatoes'. It was, in fact and in fairness, all a traditional pantomime should be, and yet I had a vague feeling that something was wrong, that an element was missing. But, as the cast came down a white staircase in glittering costumes to enthusiastic applause, it seemed the sort of pantomime I'd grown up with and which Tristan and Isolde should be content to inherit.

After so much excitement I felt in need of a stiff brandy and soda, but the eatery the children had selected for their evening's entertainment had apparently gone teetotal and alcohol was not on the menu. Once they were confronted by their mammoth burgers and fries I made my excuses, said I'd be back in a moment, and slipped into a nearby pub which was, I noticed, opposite the stage door of the Empire.

As the life-giving draught was being poured I found myself standing next to Washy and Uncle Abanazer, now out of costume, who were discussing Jim the Dame. 'Very unfriendly tonight,' Washy said. 'Locked himself in his dressing room before the show and wouldn't join us for a drink.'

'Perhaps he's had a bust-up with Molly?'

'Unlikely. Molly and Jim never have a cross word.'

'Lucky she's never found out he's been polishing Aladdin's wonderful lamp,' Abanazer said, and they both laughed.

As I asked the girl behind the bar to refill my glass, in which the tide had sunk to a dangerous low, I heard them laugh again about the Widow Twankey's voluminous bosom. 'Strapped-on polystyrene,' Abanazer was saying. 'Almost bruises me when I dance with her. Funny thing, tonight it was quite soft.'

'Perhaps she borrowed one from a blow-up woman?' Washy was laughing as I gulped my brandy and legged it back to the hamburgers. In the dark passage outside the stage door I saw a small, nimble figure in hurried retreat – Jim Diamond, who for some reason hadn't wanted to join the boys at the bar.

After I had restored the children to the Erskine-Browns' au pair I sat in the Tube on my way back to Gloucester Road and read the programme. Jim Diamond, it seemed, had started his life in industry before taking up show business. He had a busy career in clubs and turned down appearances on television. 'I only enjoy the living show,' Jim says. 'I want to have the audience where I can see them.' His photograph, without the exaggerated female make-up, showed a pale, thin-nosed, in some way disagreeable little man with a lip curled either in scorn or triumph. I wondered how such an unfriendly-looking character could become an ebullient and warm-hearted widow. Stripped of his make-up, there was something about this comic's unsmiling face which brought back memories of another meeting in totally different circumstances. It was the second time within a few weeks that I had found an old familiar face cast in a new and unexpected part.

The memory I couldn't quite grasp preyed on my mind until I was tucked up in bed. Then, as Hilda's latest historical romance dropped from her weary fingers and she turned her back on me and switched out the light, I saw the face again quite clearly but in a different setting. Not Diamond. Sparker? No, Sparksman. A logical progression. Widow Twankey had been played by Harry Sparksman, a man who had trained as a professional entertainer, if my memory was correct, not in clubs, but in Her Majesty's prisons. It was, it seemed, an interesting career change, but I thought no more of it at the time and once satisfied with my identification I fell asleep.

'The boy couldn't have done it, Mr Rumpole. Not a complicated bloody great job to that extent. His only way of getting at a safe was to dig it out of the wall and remove it bodily. He did that in a Barkingside boutique and what he found in it hardly covered the petrol. Young Denis couldn't have got into the Croydon supermarket peter. No one in our family could have.'

Uncle Fred, the experienced and cautious head of the Timson clan, had no regard for the safe-breaking talents of Denis, his nephew, and, on the whole, an unskilled recruit in the Timson enterprise. The Croydon supermarket job had been highly complicated and expertly carried out and had yielded, for its perpetrators, thousands of pounds. Peanuts Molloy was arrested as one of the lookouts after falling and twisting an ankle when chased by a night watchman during the getaway. He said he didn't know any of the skilled operators who had engaged him except Denis Timson who, he alleged, was in general charge of the operation. Denis alone, he said, had silenced the burglar alarm and deftly penetrated the lock on the safe with an oxyacetylene blowtorch.

It has to be remembered, though, that the clan Molloy had been sworn enemies of the Timson family from time immemorial. Peanuts' story sounded implausible when I met Denis Timson in the Brixton Prison interview room. A puzzled twenty-five-year-old with a shaven head and a poor attempt at a moustache, he seemed more upset by his Uncle Fred's low opinion of him than the danger of a conviction and subsequent prolonged absence from the family.

Denis's case was to come up for committal at the South London Magistrates' Court before 'Skimpy' Simpson, whose lack of success at the Bar had driven him to a job as a stipendiary beak. His nickname had been earned by the fact that he had not, within living memory, been known to splash out on a round of drinks at Pommeroy's Wine Bar.

In the usual course of events, there is no future in fighting proceedings which are only there to commit the customer to trial. I had resolved to attend solely to pour a little well-deserved contempt on the testimony of Peanuts Molloy. As I started to prepare the case, I made a note of the date of the Croydon supermarket break-in. As soon as I had done so, I consulted my diary. I turned the virgin pages, as yet unstained by notes of trials, ideas for cross-examinations, splodges of tea, or spilled glasses of Pommeroy's Very Ordinary. It was as I had thought. While some virtuoso had been at work on the Croydon safe, I had been enjoying *Aladdin* in the company of Tristan and Isolde.

'Detective Inspector Grimble, would you agree that whoever blew the safe in the Croydon supermarket did an extraordinarily skilful job?'

'Mr Rumpole, are we meant to congratulate your client on his professional skill?'

God moves in mysterious ways, and it wasn't Skimpy Simpson's fault that he was born with thin lips and a voice which sounded like the rusty hinge of a rusty gate swinging in the wind. I decided to ignore him and concentrate on a friendly chat with DI Grimble, a large, comfortable, ginger-haired officer. We had both lived, over the years, with the clan Timson and their misdoings. He was known to them as a decent and fair-minded cop, as disapproving of the younger, Panda-racing, evidence-massaging intake to the force as they were of the lack of discretion and criminal skills which marked the younger Timsons.

'I mean, the thieves were well informed. They knew that there would be a week's money in the safe.'

'They knew that, yes.'

'And wasn't there a complex burglar alarm system? You couldn't put it out of action simply by cutting wires, could you?'

'Cutting the wires would have set it off.'

'So putting the burglar alarm out of action would have required special skills?'

'It would have done.'

'Putting it out of action also stopped a clock in the office. So we know that occurred at 8.45?'

'We know that. Yes.'

'And at 9.20 young Molloy was caught as he fell while running to a getaway car.'

'That is so.'

'So this heavy safe was burned open in a little over half an hour?'

'I fail to see the relevance of this, Mr Rumpole.' Skimpy was getting restless.

'I'm sure the officer does. That shows a very high degree of technical skill, doesn't it, Detective Inspector?'

'I'd agree with that.'

'Exercised by a highly experienced peterman?'

'Who is this Mr Peterman?' Skimpy was puzzled. 'We haven't heard of him before.'

'Not *Mr* Peterman.' I marvelled at the ignorance of the basic facts of life displayed by the magistrate. 'A man expert at blowing safes, known to the trade as a "peter",' I told him and turned back to DI Grimble. 'So we're agreed that this was a highly expert piece of work?'

'It must have been done by someone who knew his job pretty well. Yes.'

'Denis Timson's record shows convictions for shoplifting, bag-snatching, and stealing a radio from an unlocked car. In all of these simple enterprises, he managed to get caught.'

'Your client's criminal record!' Skimpy looked happy for the first time. 'You're allowing that to go into evidence, are you, Mr Rumpole?'

'Certainly, sir.' I explained the obvious point. 'Because there's absolutely no indication that he was capable of blowing a safe in record time, or silencing a complicated burglar alarm, is there, Detective Inspector?'

'No. There's nothing to show anything like that in his record ...'

'Mr Rumpole.' Skimpy was looking at the clock; was he in danger of missing his usual train back home to Haywards Heath? 'Where's all this heading?'

'Back a good many years,' I told him, 'to the Sweet-Home Building Society job at Carshalton, when Harry Sparksman blew a safe so quietly that even the dogs slept through it.'

'You were in on that case, weren't you, Mr Rumpole?' Inspector Grimble was pleased to remember. 'Sparksman got five years.'

'Not one of your great successes.' Skimpy was also delighted. 'Perhaps you wasted the court's time with unnecessary questions. Have you anything else to ask this officer?'

'Not till the Old Bailey, sir. I may have thought of a few more by then.' With great satisfaction, Skimpy committed Denis Timson, a minor villain who would have had difficulty changing a fuse, let alone blowing a safe, for trial at the Central Criminal Court.

'Funny you mentioned Harry Sparksman. Do you know, the same thought occurred to me. An expert like him could've done that job in the time.'

'Great minds think alike,' I assured DI Grimble. We were washing away the memory of an hour or two before Skimpy with two pints of nourishing stout in the pub opposite the beak's court. 'You know Harry took up a new career?' I needn't have asked the question. DI Grimble had a groupie's encyclopaedic knowledge of the criminal stars.

'Oh, yes. Now a comic called Jim Diamond. Got up a concert party in the nick. Apparently gave him a taste for show business.'

'I did hear,' I took Grimble into my confidence, 'that he made a comeback for the Croydon job.' It had been a throwaway line from Uncle Fred Timson – 'I heard talk they got Harry back out of retirement' – but it was a thought worth examining.

'I heard the same. So we did a bit of checking. But Sparksman, known as Diamond, has got a cast-iron alibi.'

'Are you sure?'

'At the time when the Croydon job was done, he was performing in a pantomime. On stage nearly all the evening, it seems, playing the dame.'

'*Aladdin*,' I said, 'at the Tufnell Park Empire. It might just be worth your while to go into that alibi a little more thoroughly. I'd suggest you have a private word with Mrs Molly Diamond. It's just possible she may have noticed his attraction to Aladdin's lamp.'

'Now then, Mr Rumpole.' Grimble was wiping the froth from his lips with a neatly folded handkerchief. 'You mustn't tell me how to do my job.'

'I'm only trying to serve,' I managed to look pained, 'the interests of justice!'

'You mean, the interests of your client?'

'Sometimes they're the same thing,' I told him, but I had to admit it wasn't often.

As it happened, the truth emerged without Detective Inspector Grimble having to do much of a job. Harry had, in fact, fallen victim to a tip-tilted nose and memorable thighs; he'd left home and moved into Aladdin's Kensal Rise flat. Molly, taking a terrible revenge, blew his alibi wide open.

She had watched many rehearsals and knew every word, every gag, every nudge, wink and shrill complaint of the dame's part. She had played it to perfection to give her husband an alibi while he went back to his old job in Croydon. It all went perfectly, even though Uncle Abanazer, dancing with her, had felt an unexpected softness.

I had known, instinctively, that something was very wrong. It had, however, taken some time for me to realise what I had really seen that night at the Tufnell Park Empire. It was nothing less than an outrage to a Great British Tradition. The Widow Twankey was a woman.

DI Grimble made his arrest and the case against Denis Timson was dropped by the Crown Prosecution Service. As spring came to the Temple gardens, Hilda opened a letter in the other case which had turned on the recognition of old, familiar faces and read it out to me.

'The repointing's going well on the tower and we hope to have it finished by Easter,' Poppy Longstaff had written. 'And I have to tell you, Hilda, the oil-fired heating has changed our lives. Eric says it's like living in the tropics. Cooking supper last night I had to peel off one of my cardigans.' She Who Must Be Obeyed put down the letter from her old school friend and said, thoughtfully, 'Noblesse oblige.'

'What was that, Hilda?'

'I could tell at once that Donald Compton was a true gentleman. The sort that does good by stealth. Of course, poor old Eric thought he'd never get the tower mended, but I somehow felt that Donald wouldn't fail him. It was noblesse.'

'Perhaps it was,' I conceded, 'but in this case the noblesse was Rumpole's.'

'Rumpole! What on earth do you mean? You hardly paid to have the church tower repointed, did you?'

'In one sense, yes.'

'I can't believe that. After all the years it took you to have the bathroom decorated. What on earth do you mean about your noblesse?'

'It'd take too long to explain, old darling. Besides, I've got a conference in chambers. Tricky case of receiving stolen surgical appliances. I suppose,' I added doubtfully, 'it may lead, at some time in the distant future, to an act of charity.'

Easter came, the work on the tower was successfully completed, and I was walking back to chambers after a gruelling day down at the Bailey when I saw, wafting through the Temple cloisters, the unlikely apparition of the Revd Eric Longstaff. He chirruped a greeting and said he'd come up to consult some legal brains on the proper investment of what remained of the Church Restoration Fund.

'I'm so profoundly grateful,' he told me, 'that I decided to invite you down to the rectory last Christmas.'

'*You* decided?'

'Of course I did.'

'I thought your wife Poppy extended the invitation to She ...'

'Oh, yes. But I thought of the idea. It was the result of a good deal of hard knee-work and guidance from above. I knew you were the right man for the job.'

'What job?'

'The Compton job.'

What was this? The rector was speaking like an old con. The Coldsands caper? 'What *can* you mean?'

'I just mean that I knew you'd defended Donald Compton. In a previous existence.'

'How on earth did you know that?'

Eric drew himself up to his full, willowy height. 'I'm not a prison visitor for nothing,' he said proudly. 'I thought you were just the chap to put the fear of God into him. You were the very person to put the squeeze on the Lord of the Manor.'

'Put the squeeze on him?' Words were beginning to fail me.

'That was the idea. It came to me as a result of knee-work.'

'So you brought us down to that freezing rectory just so I could blackmail the local benefactor?'

'Didn't it turn out well!'

'May the Lord forgive you.'

'He's very forgiving.'

'Next time,' I spoke to the Man of God severely, 'the Church can do its blackmailing for itself.'

'Oh, we're quite used to that.' The rector smiled at me in what I thought was a lofty manner. 'Particularly around Christmas.'

The Problem of
Santa's Lighthouse

Edward Hoch

'You say you'd like a Christmas story this time?' old Dr
Sam Hawthorne said as he poured the drinks into fine
crystal wineglasses. 'Well, the holidays are approaching,
and as it happens I've got an adventure from December
of 1931 that fills the bill nicely. It didn't happen in Northmont, but along the coast, over toward Cape Cod …'

I'd decided to take a few days off (Dr Sam continued), and
took a drive by myself along the coast. It was something
of a treat for me, since vacations are rare for a country
doctor. But now that the Pilgrim Memorial Hospital had
opened in Northmont, some of the pressure was off. If

people couldn't reach me in an emergency, the hospital was there to minister to their ills.

So off I went in my Stutz Torpedo, promising my nurse April I'd telephone her in a few days to make certain everything was under control. It was the first week in December, but winter hadn't yet set in along the New England coast. There was no snow, and temperatures were in the forties. Along with every other part of the country, the area had been hard hit by the Depression, but once I'd passed through the old mill towns and headed north along the coast I saw less poverty.

Not far from Plymouth, a sign nailed to a tree caught my attention. *Visit Santa's Lighthouse!* it read, and although such commercial ventures to attract children are commonplace today, they were still a bit unusual in 1931. I couldn't imagine a lighthouse whose sole function was to entertain tots in the weeks before Christmas. But then I noticed that the word *Santa's* had been tacked on over the original name. It was enough to make me curious, so I turned down the road to the shore.

And there it was, sure enough: a gleaming white structure that rose from the rocky shoreline and proclaimed across its base, in foot-high wooden letters, that it was indeed Santa's Lighthouse. I parked my car next to two others and walked up the path to where a bright-faced girl of college age was selling admissions for twenty-five cents. She was wearing bright Christmassy red.

'How many?' she asked, peering down the path as if expecting me to be followed by a wife and children.

'Just one.' I took a quarter from my pocket.

'We have a special family rate of fifty cents.'

'No, I'm alone.' I pointed up at the sign. 'What's the name of this place the rest of the year?'

'You noticed we changed the sign,' she said with a grin. 'It's really Satan's Lighthouse, but there's nothing very Christmas-sounding about that. So we took the "n" off the end of Satan and moved it to the middle.'

I had to chuckle at the idea. 'Has it helped business?' 'A little. But with this Depression and gasoline twenty-five cents a gallon, we don't get many families willing to drive here from Boston or Providence.'

A bulging, padded Santa Claus appeared at the door just then, mumbling through his beard, 'Lisa, you have to do something about those kids. They're pulling the beard and kicking me!'

She sighed and turned her attention to the Santa. 'Harry, you've got to show a little patience – you can't expect me to go running in to rescue you every time they give you any trouble.'

I said, 'He's not so good at this Santa Claus business.'

'He's much better as the pirate ghost,' she agreed.

'The pirate ghost is a feature of Satan's Lighthouse?'

She gave a quick nod and offered her hand. 'I'm Lisa

Quay. That's my brother, Harry. There's a legend that goes with this place – I guess it's why our father bought it.'

'Buried treasure.'

'How'd you guess? Pirates are supposed to have put up a false light here to lure ships onto the rocks and loot them, just as they once did off the coast of Cornwall. That's why it was called Satan's Lighthouse. When a real lighthouse was built years later, the local people called it by the same name. But of course there aren't pirates any more – except when my brother puts on his costume.'

I introduced myself and she told me more about the region. She was an open, unassuming young woman who seemed more than capable of taking care of herself – and her brother, from what I'd seen. 'Is your father here, too?' I asked.

She shook her head. 'Daddy's in prison.'

'Oh?'

'He was convicted of some sort of fraud last year. I never fully understood it, and I don't believe he was guilty, but he refused to defend himself. He has another year to serve before he's eligible for parole.'

'So you and your brother are keeping this place going in his absence.'

'That's about it. Now you know my life story, Dr Hawthorne.'

'Call me Sam. I'm not that much older than you.'

Four unruly children came out of the lighthouse, shepherded by a frustrated Santa Claus. I watched while they piled into a waiting car and drove off with their parents. 'Anyone else inside now?' Lisa asked her brother.

'No, it's empty.'

'You're not making any money by my standing here,' I decided, plunking down the quarter I was still holding. 'I'll have a ticket.'

'Come on,' Harry Quay said. 'I'll show you through.' The lighthouse was a slender whitewashed structure with rectangular sides that tapered toward the top, where a railing and walkway surrounded the light itself. I followed Quay up the iron staircase that spiralled through the centre of the structure. The padded Santa suit didn't slow him down and he made the first landing well ahead of me. I was short of breath and welcomed the pause when he led me to a room that had been converted into a Santa's workshop.

'We bring the kids up here and give them inexpensive little toys,' he explained. 'Then we go the rest of the way up to the light.'

'What's the room used for the rest of the year?'

'Originally it was the sleeping quarters for the lighthouse crew – generally a keeper and his wife. Of course, Lisa and I don't live here ourselves. We use the room for the pirate's den when it's not Christmas.'

I glanced at the spiral staircase, anxious to get the rest of the climbing behind me. 'Let's see the top.'

We went up another dozen feet to the next level, where a rolltop desk and wooden filing cabinet had been outfitted with signs indicating it was Santa's office. The nautical charts of Cape Cod Bay on the walls were festooned with streamers proclaiming a landing area for Santa's reindeer-powered sleigh. There were powerful binoculars and a telescope for observing passing ships, and a two-way radio for receiving weather reports or S.O.S. messages.

'I have to watch the kids every minute up here,' Harry Quay said. 'Some of this equipment is valuable.'

'I'm surprised it's still here if the lighthouse is no longer in use.'

'My father kept them for some reason. He used to sit up here at night sometimes. It was a hobby of his, I suppose. That's why he bought the place.'

I gestured toward the ceiling of the little office. 'Does the light up above still operate?'

'I doubt it. I haven't tried it myself.'

We climbed the rest of the way to the circular outside walkway that went around the light itself. A metal railing allowed me a handhold, but one could easily slip beneath it and fall to the ground. 'You don't bring the kids up here, do you?'

'One at a time, with me holding their hand. I'm very careful.'

I had to admit it was a magnificent view. On the bay side the land fell away rapidly to the water's edge, and as far as I could see the chill waters were casting up rippling whitecaps before the stiff ocean breeze. The curve of Cape Cod itself was clearly visible from this high up, and I could even make out the opposite shoreline some twenty miles across the bay.

But at this time of the year night came early and the sun was already low in the western sky. 'I'd better get going if I want to reach Boston tonight,' I said.

'Why go that far? There are plenty of places to stay around Plymouth.'

We went back downstairs and met Lisa at the workshop level. 'Did you enjoy the view? Isn't it spectacular?'

'It certainly is,' I agreed. 'You should double your prices.'

'No one comes as it is,' she replied with a touch of sadness.

'If the light still works, turn it on! Bring in some customers in the early evening.'

'Oh, the coast guard would never allow that.' She bustled about the workroom, picking up a few candy wrappers dropped by the children, retrieving a reel of fishing line and a set of jacks from one corner. 'You find the darnedest things at the end of the day.'

'Your brother says there are some places I could stay in the Plymouth area.'

'Sure. The Plymouth Rock is a nice old place, and the rooms are clean.' She turned to her brother. 'Let's close up for the night.'

'I'd better make sure everything's shut upstairs,' Harry said.

'I'll go with you.'

I started down the spiral staircase to the ground floor. I waited a few minutes, thinking they'd be following soon, but I became restless. The lighthouse had been a pleasant diversion, but I was anxious to move on.

'Wait a minute!' Lisa Quay called out as I started down the path to my car. She was at one of the middle windows, and I paused while she came down to meet me.

'I didn't mean to leave without saying goodbye,' I told her, 'but it's getting dark and I should be on my way.'

'At least wait for Harry. He's taking off his Santa Claus suit. He'll be down in a minute.'

I strolled back with her while she closed up the fold-away ticket booth and stowed it inside the lighthouse doorway. 'If this weather holds out, you should get some crowds before Christmas.'

'I hope so,' she said. 'Those four kids you saw were the only customers we had all afternoon.'

'Maybe you could offer a special group-rate for—'

'What's that?' she asked suddenly, hurrying back outside. 'Harry?' she called out, looking up. 'Is that you?'

There was some sort of noise from above us and then Lisa Quay screamed. I looked up in time to see a figure falling from the circular walkway at the top of the lighthouse. I sprang aside, pulling her with me, as Harry Quay's body hit the ground where we'd been standing.

Lisa turned away screaming, her hands covering her face. I hurried over to her brother, my mind racing through the possibilities of getting fast help if he was still alive.

Then I saw the handle of the dagger protruding from between his ribs and I knew that help was useless.

'I don't believe in ghosts,' she said quite rationally as we waited for the police to arrive. I'd used the lighthouse radio to call the coast guard, who promised to contact the state police for us. While I was inside, I'd looked in both rooms and even inside a little storeroom, but the lighthouse was empty. There was nothing on the walkway to indicate anyone else had been there, nothing on the spiral staircase to point to an unseen visitor.

'We don't have to believe in ghosts,' I told her. 'There's a logical explanation. There has to be. Have you ever seen that dagger before?'

'Yes. It's part of his pirate costume. The storeroom—'

'I checked the storeroom. I saw the costume hanging there. No one was hiding.'

'Well, I don't believe in ghosts,' she said again.

'The police will be here soon.'

She fastened her hand on my arm. 'You won't leave, will you? You won't leave before they come?'

'Of course not.' I'd moved her away from her brother's body, so she'd be spared the sight while we waited for the police. I could see she was close to hysteria and might need my professional services at any moment.

'Without your testimony they might try to say I killed him,' she said. 'Even though I had no reason to.'

'I'm sure they wouldn't say that,' I tried to assure her.

'But no one else is here! Don't you see how it looks?'

'You were down on the ground with me when he was stabbed. I'll testify to that.'

'Suppose I rigged up some sort of device to throw the knife at him when he stepped out onto the walkway.'

I shook my head. 'I was up there with him shortly before he was killed. And I went up there again a few moments ago. There was no device, and nothing left over from one. There was nothing at all on that walkway.'

'Then what killed him? Who killed him?'

Before I could respond, we saw the headlights of two police cars and an ambulance cutting through the early darkness. I had plenty of time to tell my story then, and

Lisa told hers. They walked around with their flashlights, examining the body, asking questions, going through the motions. But it was clear that they didn't want to deal with a pirate ghost, much less any sort of impossible crime. I fondly wished for old Sheriff Lens back in Northmont. At least he could keep an open mind about such things.

'Did your brother have any enemies?' one officer asked Lisa.

'No, none at all. I can't imagine anyone wishing him harm.'

'Can you tell me why he's wearing this false beard?'

'He'd been playing Santa Claus for the children. He was changing out of his costume when it happened.'

The officer, a burly man named Springer, turned to me next. 'Dr Hawthorne?'

'That's correct.'

'You say you were just passing through, not bound for any particular place?'

'Just a little vacation,' I explained. 'I practice in North-mont, near the Connecticut state line. The sign attracted me, and I stopped for an hour or so.'

'Ever know the deceased or his sister before?'

'No.'

He sighed and glanced at his pocket watch. Perhaps he hadn't had supper yet. 'Well, if both of you are telling the truth, it looks like an accident to me. Somehow he slipped and fell on the knife up there, and then toppled off the walkway. Or else he killed himself.'

'That couldn't—' Lisa started to say, but I nudged her into silence. The officer seemed not to notice.

As the body was being taken away, she said, 'I'll have to notify Father.'

'How do you go about that? Where's his prison?'

'Near Boston. I'll phone a message tonight and go there tomorrow to see him.'

I made a decision. 'I'd like to go with you.'

'What for?'

'I've had a little experience in solving crimes like this. I may be able to help you.'

'But there are no suspects! Where would you begin?'

'With your father,' I said.

I slept surprisingly well in my room at the Plymouth Rock, and awoke refreshed. After a quick breakfast, I picked up Lisa at the small house in town she'd shared with her brother. 'The police called this morning,' she said. 'They want us both to come in and make statements about what happened.'

'We'll do it this afternoon,' I decided. 'Let's see your father first.'

'What do you hope to learn from him?'

'The reason why he's in prison, among other things. You seem reluctant to talk about it.'

'I'm not reluctant at all!' she bristled. 'Until now I didn't really feel it was any of your business. Daddy brought us up after Mother died. What happened to him was a terrible thing. He's in prison for a crime he didn't commit.'

'You said something about a fraud.'

'I'll let him tell you about it.'

Because of his son's death, we were both allowed to see Ronald Quay together. He was a thin man, who looked as if he might have aged overnight. His pale complexion had already taken on the look of endless incarceration, even though Lisa said he'd been locked up for only a year. She cried when he was led into the room, and the guard stood by awkwardly as they embraced.

'This is Dr Sam Hawthorne,' she told her father. 'He was at the lighthouse with us when it happened.'

He wanted details and I told him everything I knew. He sat across the table, merely shaking his head.

'I've done a little amateur detective work back in Northmont,' I told him. 'I thought I might be able to help out here.'

'How?'

'By asking the right questions.' I paused, sizing up the man almost as I would diagnose a patient's illness, and then I said, 'You're in prison for committing a crime, and now the crime of murder has apparently been committed against your son. I wonder if there could be a relationship between those two crimes.'

'I don't—' He shook his head.

'I know it seems impossible that anyone could have killed Harry, but if someone did they had to have a motive.'

'He didn't have an enemy in the world,' Lisa insisted.

'Perhaps he was killed not for what he was like but for what he was doing,' I suggested.

'You mean playing Santa Claus?'

'You said he played a pirate, too. And he was struck down with a pirate's dagger.'

'Who could possibly—?'

I interrupted her with another question for her father. 'Were you engaged in any sort of illegal activity at the lighthouse?'

'Certainly not,' he answered without hesitation. 'I've maintained my innocence of these charges from the beginning.'

'Then the fraud charges somehow involved the lighthouse?'

'Only in the most general way,' Lisa replied. 'At one point we tried to set up a corporation and sell shares of stock. A Boston man went to the police and accused my father of fraud because Daddy claimed he had a million dollars to build an amusement park.'

'Did you ever claim that?' I asked him.

'No! Harry suggested once that we put in one of those miniature golf courses that are all the rage, but I was against even that. Certainly no one ever mentioned a million dollars.'

'They must have had evidence of fraud.'

He looked at his hands. 'A stock prospectus we had printed, just for test purposes. It wasn't supposed to get out. Lisa can tell you we don't even own much land around the lighthouse— We couldn't have built an amusement park there even if we'd wanted to.'

Lisa sighed. 'That's exactly the argument the prosecutor used to convict you, Daddy.'

I was aware that he'd neatly avoided the main thrust of my question by bringing up the fraud conviction. 'Forget the fraud charges for the moment, Mr Quay. What about other activities at the lighthouse?'

'I don't know what you mean,' he said, but his eyes shifted away.

'The two-way radio. The powerful binoculars. The telescope. They were used to locate and contact ships offshore, weren't they?'

'Why would I—?' he began, then changed his mind. 'All right. You seem to know a great deal.'

'What were they landing at the lighthouse? Illegal whiskey from Canada, I imagine.'

Lisa's eyes widened. 'Daddy!'

'I needed money from somewhere, Lisa. Using that lighthouse for pirates and Santa Clauses was a losing proposition from the beginning.'

'You told Dr Hawthorne there'd been no illegal activity there.'

'Prohibition is an unjust and unpopular law. I don't consider that I acted illegally in helping to circumvent it.'

'What happened after you went to prison?' I asked. 'Did Harry continue the bootlegging activities?'

'He knew nothing about it,' Quay insisted.

'And yet the radio and telescope are still in place, a year later.'

'He was sentimental about moving them,' Lisa explained. 'He wanted everything just as it was for when Daddy came back.'

'You must have dealt with someone on this bootlegging operation, Mr Quay. Couldn't that man have contacted Harry and struck a deal with him after your imprisonment?'

Ronald Quay was silent for a moment, considering the possibility. 'I suppose so,' he admitted at last. 'That would be like him. And it would be like Harry to accept the deal without telling anyone.'

'I need the name, Mr Quay.'

'I'm—'

'The name of the man you dealt with. The name of the person who might have contacted your son to continue with the setup. Because that might be the name of his murderer.'

'Paul Lane,' he said at last. 'That's the name you want.' The words had been an effort for him to speak.

'Who is he? Where can we find him?'

'He owns some seafood restaurants along the coast. I can give you an address in Boston.'

As we parked my Stutz Torpedo along the Boston docks a few hours later, Lisa said, 'Sam, how come you're not married?'

'I've never met the right woman at the right time, I guess.'

'I want to ask you something – a very great favour.'

'What is it?'

'Could you stay here with me – until after Harry's funeral? I don't think I could get through it alone.'

'When–?'

'Day after tomorrow. You could leave by noon if you wanted to. They'll let Daddy come down from prison with a guard, and there'll be some aunts and uncles. That's all. We're not a big family.'

'Let me think about it. Maybe I can.'

Lane's Lobsters was a seafood restaurant that also

sold live lobsters for boiling at home. A grey-haired man behind the lobster tank told us Paul Lane's office was up-stairs. We climbed the rickety steps to the second floor and found him sitting behind a cluttered desk. He puffed on a fat cigar that gave him the look of a minor politician.

'What can I do for you?' he asked, removing the cigar from his mouth.

'We're interested in some lobsters,' I said.

'The retail business is downstairs. I just handle whole-sale up here.' He gestured toward an open ice-chest full of dead lobsters.

'That's what we want – wholesale.'

He squinted at Lisa. 'Don't I know you?'

'You may know my brother. Harry Quay.'

Paul Lane was no good at hiding his reaction. After the first shock of surprise he tried to cover it with a denial, but I pressed on. 'You run a bootlegging operation, Lane, and you involved her father and brother in it.'

'Go to hell! Get outa here!'

'We want to talk. Somebody killed her brother last evening.'

'I read the papers. They say it was an accident.'

'I was there. I call it murder.'

Paul Lane's lip twisted in a sneer. 'Is that so? If you two were alone with him, then you must have killed him.'

I leaned on the desk between us. 'We didn't come here

to play games, Mr Lane. I think you approached Harry after his father went to prison on that fraud rap. You wanted to continue bringing your Canadian whiskey ashore at Satan's Lighthouse, and you needed Harry's co-operation. Isn't that right?'

He got up from his desk and deliberately closed the lid on the ice-chest. 'I don't know what you're talking about, mister.'

As a lobsterman or a bootlegger, he might have been pretty good, but just then he was being a bit too obvious. When he sat down again I lifted the lid and picked up one of the cold lobsters.

'What in hell are you doing?' he bellowed, coming out of his chair.

I turned the lobster over. Its insides had been hollowed out to make room for a slim bottle of whiskey. 'Neat,' I said. 'I'll bet that's a popular take-out item at your restaurants.'

Before I realised what was happening, his fist caught me on the side of the head. I stumbled back against the ice-chest as Lisa screamed. Two tough-looking seamen barged in, attracted by the noise. 'Get them!' Lane ordered. 'Both of them!'

I was still clutching the dead lobster and I shoved it into the nearest man's face. 'Run!' I shouted to Lisa. Lane was out from behind his desk, trying to stop her, when I shoved him aside and followed her out the door. Then all three of them were after us and I felt one beefy hand grab at my shoulder. We made it halfway down the stairs before they caught us, and I tripped and stumbled the rest of the way to the ground floor, landing hard on my chest.

I looked up and saw one of the men take out a knife. Then I saw someone from the restaurant grab his wrist.

I recognised Springer, the state police officer who had questioned us. 'Having a little trouble here, Dr Hawthorne?' he asked.

I'd cracked a rib falling down the stairs, and while it was being taped up Springer explained that he'd gone to the prison to question Ronald Quay, arriving just as we were leaving. 'You seemed in such a hurry I decided to follow along. You led me here.'

The Boston police and agents of the Prohibition Bureau had taken over Paul Lane's operation, seizing hundreds of barrels of good Canadian whiskey. My last glimpse of Lane was when a cop led him away in handcuffs. 'Did he kill my brother?' Lisa asked.

'Not personally, but he probably ordered it done. I can't name the actual killer, but I can give you a description of him and tell you how I think the murder was committed.'

'I hope you're not going to say somebody threw the knife from the rocks all the way to the top of that lighthouse,' Springer said.

'No,' I agreed. 'It's much too tall for that. And that pirate dagger is too unbalanced to have been fired from a crossbow or anything similar. The killer was right there with Harry when he died.'

'But that's impossible!' Lisa insisted.

'No, it isn't. There was one place in that lighthouse we never searched, one place where the killer could have been hidden – the rolltop desk in the office on the top floor.'

'But that's absurd!' Lisa said. 'It's hardly big enough for a child!'

'Exactly – a child. Or someone dressed as a child. Remember that carload of children that arrived just before me? Didn't you think it odd the parents remained in the car – especially since the lighthouse offered a family rate? Four children came out, but I'm willing to bet that five children went in.'

Lisa's eyes widened. 'My lord, I think you're right!'

'One stayed behind, hidden in that rolltop desk. And when Harry came back upstairs to close up, he did his job. He was a hit man hired by Paul Lane, who'd had a falling-out with your brother over the bootlegging business. I think we'll find enough evidence in Lane's records to verify that.'

Springer was frowning. 'You're telling us a child was the hit man?'

'Or someone dressed as a child,' I said. 'Someone small – maybe a midget.'

'A midget!'

'What better hit man to kill a Santa Claus than a midget dressed as a small child? Five children entered the lighthouse but only four came out. No one thought of the missing child. The supposed parents drove away, leaving a hidden killer awaiting his opportunity.'

'All right,' Springer said with a nod. 'If Lane has a midget on his payroll it should be easy enough to discover.' He started out and then paused at the door with a slight smile. 'I checked up on you. Sheriff Lens back in Northmont says you're a pretty fair detective.'

When he had gone, Lisa Quay said simply, 'Thank you. It won't bring him back, but at least I know what happened.'

Two days later I was at Lisa Quay's side as her brother was buried beneath the barren December trees of the Plymouth cemetery. As we were walking to the car, Springer intercepted us. 'I thought you'd like to know that we have a line on a very short man who worked as a waiter last year in Paul Lane's New Bedford lobster house. We're trying to locate him now.'

'Good luck,' I said. 'I'm heading home today.'

My car was back at the funeral parlour and I said goodbye to Lisa Quay there. 'Thanks again,' she said. 'For everything, Sam.'

I'd been driving about an hour when I saw the boy fishing off a bridge over a narrow creek. My first thought was that December wasn't likely to be a good fishing month.

My second thought was that I'd made a terrible mistake. I pulled the car off the road and sat for a long time staring at nothing at all. Finally I started the motor and made a U-turn, heading back the way I had come.

It was late afternoon when Santa's Lighthouse came into view, much as it had been that first day I saw the place. Lisa's car was parked nearby, but no others. The lighthouse was still closed to visitors. I pulled in next to her car and got out, walking up the path to the doorway. She must have heard the car and seen me from the window, because she opened the door with a smile.

'You've come back, Sam.'

'Just for a little bit,' I told her. 'Can we talk?'

'About what?' She was flirting, seductive.

'About Harry's murder.'

Her face changed. 'Have they found the midget?'

I shook my head. 'They'll never find the midget because there never was one. I made a mistake.'

'What are you talking about?'

'We kept saying there were no suspects, but of course there always was one suspect. Not the least likely person but the most likely one. You killed your brother, Lisa.'

'You're insane!' she flared, trying to close the door on

me. I easily blocked it with my foot, and after a moment she relaxed and I stepped inside.

'The more I thought about it, the more impossible the midget hit man became. Those kids were raising a fuss, pulling Santa's beard and otherwise calling attention to themselves. That's hardly the sort of thing our killer would have allowed. The success of his scheme as I imagined it depended upon their group being unnoticed and uncounted.' Lisa stood with her arms folded, pretending to humour me.

'Then, too, there was the matter of the murder weapon. A hit man would certainly bring his own weapon, not rely on finding a pirate dagger in a storeroom.'

'Third point: how did the killer lure Harry out onto that walkway, especially when he was still removing his costume and had the beard on?'

'He might have been stabbed in the office below,' Lisa said, her voice a mere whisper.

I shook my head. 'No midget could have carried Harry's body up that ladder. He went up there by himself, with his murderer, and with the fake beard still on, because it was someone he trusted.'

'You're forgetting I was with you when he was killed.'

'Correction – you were with me when his body fell from the walkway. An hour ago on the road I passed a boy fishing off a bridge. And I remembered you picking up a reel of fishing line in the workroom. It hadn't been left by a child at all. You simply needed it for your scheme. You went back upstairs, called your brother up to the walkway on some pretext, stabbed him, and left his body right at the edge where it could easily be slid beneath the railing. You tied one end of the fishing line to his body and dropped the other end over the side of the lighthouse to the ground. It was nearly dark at the time, and I didn't see it when I went out. You called me back because you needed me for your alibi. I suppose you'd been waiting for days for the right person to happen along just at dusk. You pulled on the line and Harry's body rolled off the catwalk, nearly hitting us as it fell to the ground.'

'If that's true, what happened to the fishing line?'

'I missed it in the dim light when I examined the body. Then when I went upstairs to radio for help, you simply untied it from the body and hid it away.'

'Why would I kill my own brother?'

'Because you discovered he was responsible for sending your father to prison. It was Harry who printed that phoney stock prospectus and tried to defraud investors with dreams of an amusement park. Your father was covering up for him. When you learned about that, and learned that Harry was involved in the bootlegging scheme with Paul Lane, it was more than you could bear.'

The fight had gone out of her. 'At first I couldn't believe

the things he'd done – letting Daddy go to prison for his crime! And then this thing with Lane! I—'

'How did it happen?' I asked quietly.

Her voice was sombre. 'I waited a week for someone like you to come by – someone alone. Then I called him up there and gave him one last chance. I told him he had to confess to the police and get Daddy out of prison or I'd kill him. He laughed and made a grab for the dagger and I stabbed him. I used the fishing line just like you said. It was strong but thin, and almost invisible in the fading light.' She looked away. 'I thought I was lucky you came along, but I guess luck doesn't run in the family.'

'You have to tell Springer,' I said. 'He's looking for that waiter. If you let an innocent man go to prison, you'd be as wrong as your brother was.'

'All that planning,' she said. 'For nothing.'

'That was how it ended,' Dr Sam concluded. 'I wasn't particularly proud of my part in the affair, and I never told the folks back in Northmont about it. When my nurse April asked about the tape on my ribs I told her I'd fallen down. But by the time Christmas came we had snow, and it was a merry holiday for all of us. Then early the following year came that business at the cemetery – which *didn't* involve a ghost. But that's for next time.'

Credits

'The Man with the Sack' by Margery Allingham, reprinted by permission of Peters Fraser & Dunlop (*www.petersfraserdunlop.com*) on behalf of the Estate of Margery Allingham.

'The Adventure of the Red Widow' by Adrian Conan Doyle & John Dickson Carr from *The Exploits of Sherlock Holmes* © The Estate of Adrian Conan Doyle and the Estate of John Dickson Carr, 1952. Grateful acknowledgement is made to Conan Doyle Estate Ltd and David Higham Associates.

'Camberwell Crackers' © Anthony Horowitz, 2018.

'A Problem in White' by Nicholas Blake, reprinted by permission of Peters Fraser & Dunlop (*www.petersfraserdunlop.com*) on behalf of The Estate of Nicholas Blake.

'Loopy' by Ruth Rendell from *The New Girlfriend and Other Stories* © Kingsmarkham Enterprises Ltd, 1985, is reprinted by permission of United Agents.

'Morse's Greatest Mystery' © Colin Dexter, 1987. Reproduced with permission of the Licensor through PLSclear.

'The Jar of Ginger' © Gladys Mitchell, 1950, reprinted by permission of the author, care of Gregory and Company.

'Rumpole and the Old Familiar Faces' © John Mortimer, 2001, London. Reprinted by permission of Penguin Books Ltd.

'The Problem of Santa's Lighthouse' © Edward D. Hoch, 1931, reprinted by permission of the Estate care of Sternig & Byrne Literary Agency.

While every effort has been made to contact copyright-holders of each story, the author and publishers would be grateful for information where they have been unable to trace them, and would be glad to make amendments in further editions.